I0694562

The Door Back To You

Ava Larkson

Copyright © 2025
Published by Pure Joy Press
All rights reserved.

No part of this book may be reproduced, stored in a
retrieval system, or transmitted in any form or by any
means—electronic, mechanical, photocopying,
recording, or otherwise—without prior written
permission of the publisher, except in the case of brief
quotations used in reviews or articles.

This is a work of fiction.
Names, characters, places, and events are the product of
the author's imagination. Any resemblance to actual
persons, living or dead, or to actual events or locales, is
purely coincidental.

For information, email: press.pure.joy@gmail.com

ISBN (paperback): 978-1-997714-21-7
ISBN (hardcover): 978-1-997714-19-4
ISBN (eBook): 978-1-997714-20-0

Printed in the United States of America.

Author's Note

When I first imagined this story, it began with a simple feeling—the way a familiar smell can pull you home, even when you're not sure you belong there anymore. For me, that scent has always been something warm from the oven. Something made with care. Something shared.

The Door Back To You is a love letter to second chances, to quiet courage, and to the people who show up for us when life gets messy. It's about rebuilding—brick by brick, recipe by recipe—and finding comfort in unexpected places.

If you've ever had to start over, if you've ever been afraid to open a new door, or if you've ever discovered strength you didn't know you had, this story is for you.

Thank you for turning these pages and walking through this door with me.

—Ava Larkson

*For the ones who always show up—
even when the door sticks, squeaks,
or needs a little extra push.*

*"Sometimes the smallest push
opens the biggest chapter."*

CHAPTER 1

Ava Carson hadn't driven down Maple Ridge's main street in almost ten years, but somehow it felt exactly the same—and completely different.

The same weathered brick buildings.

The same maple trees lining the sidewalks.

The same hand-painted signs that looked charming only if you weren't from here.

But the town felt quieter now. Like someone had turned the volume down on a place that used to hum with morning chatter and the smell of fresh dough.

Her fingers tightened on the steering wheel as she eased her car into a parking spot across from the bakery. Her grandmother's bakery. The building she had promised—out loud, in a moment of late-night courage—she would come back and save.

She just hadn't realized how much saving it would need. The sight of it stole her breath.

"Wow," she whispered. "You look... rough."

The Buttered Biscuit Bakery used to glow with soft yellow paint and cheerful blue window trim, like something out of an old postcard. Now the paint had faded into a tired beige. A long crack split through one of the front windows. The awning sagged, the fabric bleached from too many summers.

Ava stepped out of her car and crossed the quiet street, the familiar creak of the old crosswalk sign echoing in her ears— another memory.

She paused at the door.

The wooden frame, once sturdy and freshly varnished, was chipped and worn. A rusted bell hung above it, tilted to one side like it had given up. She touched the cool metal of the handle, feeling an unexpected tremble in her hand.

She could almost hear her grandmother's voice behind her. *Go on, sweetheart. Push.*

Ava exhaled and pressed the door open.

The smell hit her first—dust, old sugar, and something faintly metallic. Not at all the warm, buttery cloud she remembered floating through as a little girl. The lights flickered weakly when she found the switch.

The bakery looked like it had frozen in time... and then quietly fallen apart.

Flour bins sat open and clumped. A rolling pin lay on the floor near the counter, forgotten. Chair legs stuck out at odd angles like someone had been halfway through cleaning up and never came back. The pastry display case was dusty and empty, with a tiny smiley-face sticker still stuck to the glass—a remnant of her grandmother's habit of making everything unnecessarily cheerful.

Something inside her chest pinched.

"I'm here now," she whispered to the empty room. "I'll fix it. I promise."

She took another step forward.

A soft crack sounded above her.

She froze.

Another crack. Louder.

Ava slowly lifted her gaze toward the ceiling—
—and a ceiling tile dropped straight toward her head.
She gasped and stumbled backward just in time as it crashed onto the counter, exploding into a cloud of dust and debris.

Ava stared at it, heart pounding, dust settling in her hair and eyelashes.

"Well," she breathed, coughing. "Welcome home."

Ava brushed dust off her shoulders, coughing until her eyes watered. For a moment, all she could hear was her own heartbeat thudding in her ears.

Then a floorboard creaked behind her.

Ava stiffened.

Someone was standing in the doorway.

She turned slowly, half expecting another ceiling tile to drop —or worse, a raccoon to leap out of the shadows.

Instead, she found him.

Elias Hart.

The last person she wanted to see. The last person she expected to see.

Tall, broad-shouldered, still wearing that maddeningly calm expression that had once infuriated her and comforted her in equal measure. His dark hair was a little longer now, his jaw a little scruffier, but his eyes... those hadn't changed. Warm brown. Steady. Too steady.

They locked onto her, widening slightly as he took in the dust in her hair and the shattered tile on the counter.

"Ava?" His voice was low, familiar in a way that made something twist beneath her ribs. "Are you... okay?"

Of course he would show up now—in the first five minutes of her being back in town, looking like she'd crawled through a chimney.

Perfect.
She swallowed hard. "Yeah. Ceiling tried to kill me, but other

than that? Just peachy."

A corner of his mouth lifted. Not quite a smile. More like he was remembering something — a version of her from before everything went wrong.

Elias stepped inside, boots crunching on plaster dust. "Let me help you—"

"No." She held up a hand, even though it trembled slightly. "I'm fine. Really."

He hesitated, then nodded once. "Your grandmother would be happy you came back."

The words hit harder than she expected.

Ava looked away, blinking. "Yeah," she whispered. "I hope so."

For a moment, neither of them spoke. Dust floated gently through a beam of afternoon light between them, making the bakery look like some forgotten snow globe.

Finally Elias shifted. "I'm working down the street now. If you need anything—tools, extra hands—just... come find me."

She didn't trust her voice enough to answer, so she just nodded.

He offered one last searching look, then stepped back out into the fading daylight.
The silence that followed felt heavier than the ceiling tile.
Ava let out a shaky breath.

"Great," she muttered. "Day one, and I've already run into the ghost of heartbreak past."

She brushed the last of the dust off her shirt and looked around the ruins of the bakery.

"Okay," she whispered to the empty room. "Let's try this again."

CHAPTER 2

Ava brushed dust from her sleeve and took a slow breath, trying to steady her nerves. The remains of the fallen ceiling tile still coated the counter like gray snow, its powdery grit clinging to her hands. Something inside her chest gave a nervous flutter.

If the ceiling was already giving up on her... what else was? She stepped deeper into the bakery, each footfall stirring up tiny clouds of dust. The familiar creak of the wooden floorboards echoed around her—older, louder, and somehow sadder than she remembered.

"Okay," she whispered to herself. "Let's see what I'm working with."

She found a clipboard resting on the wall by the back hallway, still hanging from a rusted nail. Her grandmother's handwriting curled across the top of the yellowed page.

To-Do List
Ava smiled faintly... until she read the items:
– Replace lights
 – Fix sink leak
 – Clean storage room
 – Find electrician
 – Order flour
 – Repair front window
– Ask Declan about ceiling

Ava blinked.

"Ask Declan about the ceiling?"

The name tugged at something familiar... but she couldn't quite place it. A classmate? A neighbor? Someone who used to help at the bakery?

She pulled the clipboard off the wall and carried it with her as she made her way toward the back. The hallway was darker than she remembered, the overhead light flickering with an erratic buzz.

Great. Add lightbulbs to the list.

She pushed open the door to the kitchen.

And stopped.

The once-busy workspace—where she'd rolled dough beside her grandmother on sleepy Saturday mornings—looked like a bakery crime scene.

Flour dusted the stainless-steel counters like frost. Mixing bowls were stacked in teetering towers. A pot sat abandoned on the stove, long-since empty but still smelling faintly of burnt sugar. The refrigerator hummed unevenly, rattling every few seconds like it was fighting for its life.

"Oh boy…" Ava whispered, gently touching the dusty counter. "You really fell apart without us, didn't you?"

She moved slowly through the space, opening cabinets, checking drawers, taking inventory.

Several knobs were loose. One drawer stuck halfway and refused to budge. A cupboard door dangled by a single hinge. Ava sighed.

She flipped to a new page on the clipboard and began writing:
— **Hinges**
— **Drawer track**
— **Deep clean kitchen**
— **Replace fridge gasket?**
— **Possibly entire fridge?!**
— **Ceiling repair (urgent)**

She clicked the pen closed and rested both hands on the counter, letting her head drop forward.

It was worse than she expected.

Much worse.

And yet... beneath the exhaustion creeping into her bones, she felt something else too.

Hope.

Because this was still her grandmother's bakery.

Still the place where she'd learned to braid challah and whisk batter and laugh until her stomach hurt. Still the place where her grandmother had pressed a warm, flour-dusted kiss to her forehead every Saturday morning.

"If anyone's going to bring you back to life," Ava murmured, "it's me."

A soft thud came from somewhere behind her.

She froze.

Another sound—like a shuffle.

Her pulse jumped.

"Hello?" she called, stepping toward the walk-in pantry door.

No answer.

Ava wrapped her hand around the handle and slowly pulled it open.

The dark pantry stared back at her, shelves lined with near-empty jars and expired spices. Nothing moved.

Just her imagination.

She exhaled and started to close the door—
—and a large shadow shifted behind the flour sacks.

Ava jerked back with a small gasp.

A pair of round, dark eyes peeked out from behind a stack of bags.

A squirrel.

A plump, very comfortable-looking squirrel.

Sitting inside her pantry.

Holding a stolen biscotti.

Ava blinked. "Oh, you've got to be kidding me."

The squirrel blinked back—as if offended she'd interrupted its snack—then darted between two shelves and disappeared into a hole chewed through the drywall.

Ava pressed a hand to her forehead.

"Add exterminator to the list," she muttered.

She shut the pantry door and leaned against it, laughing in disbelief.

The bakery was falling apart. The ceiling was collapsing. A rogue squirrel had apparently taken up residence. And the mysterious Declan—whoever he was—was apparently the only person who knew anything about the ceiling.

Ava picked up the clipboard again.

"Tomorrow," she said firmly. "Tomorrow, I find Declan."

She looked around at the shadows settling across the empty kitchen, dust glimmering in the fading afternoon light.

"Because I can't do this alone."

She took one last breath, grabbed her purse, and headed for the front door.

Outside, the sun was dipping behind Maple Ridge's rooftops, turning the street gold.

Ava locked the bakery behind her.

Tomorrow would be the real beginning.

And little did she know... Declan Hayes was about to turn her plans—and her heart—completely upside down.

CHAPTER 3

Ava blinked through the dust as it slowly drifted down around her, settling on her clothes and eyelashes. The ceiling tile lay shattered on the counter like a warning.

She brushed debris from her hair.
"Okay," she muttered. "Not ideal."

A floorboard creaked behind her.

Ava froze.

She turned—and nearly collided with a tall man filling the doorway. He stepped inside like he owned the oxygen in the room.

He was broad-shouldered, work-booted, and dusted with sawdust like it was part of his wardrobe. His gray T-shirt clung to a toned chest, and he held a tape measure hooked to his belt. Dark hair curled slightly at his temples, as if humidity—or sweat—had given up taming it.

He looked like a walking construction hazard.

His voice was low, gravelly.
"You shouldn't be standing under that part of the ceiling."

Ava blinked. "Thanks. Really helpful now that it's already dropped on me."

He looked at the shattered tile, then at her, completely unfazed.

"You didn't get hit?"

"No."

"You're lucky."

"I'm aware."

He nodded once, a quiet, assessing gesture.
Then he walked right past her, boots thudding on the worn floorboards.

"I'm Declan Hayes," he said. "The contractor you called."

Ava stiffened. She had expected… someone older. Someone with a clipboard. Someone with less attitude.
She crossed her arms.

"I didn't think you'd be here this fast."

"I was already in town," he replied, running a hand along the cracked window frame. "Figured I'd swing by before the whole building caves in."

She frowned. "Is that supposed to be a joke?"

"No."

Ava exhaled sharply.
Great. A man with zero sense of humor and the emotional warmth of a snow shovel.
Declan kept moving, inspecting everything: the walls, the ceiling, the pastry case, the floorboards. His deep brown eyes missed nothing.

"So," Ava said, trying to reclaim the moment, "I have a vision for the place."

Declan actually snorted.
"A vision."

"Yes, a vision. I want it to feel bright and charming again. Fresh paint, new trim, maybe open shelving—"

He held up a hand.
"You can't start with paint."

"I wasn't starting, I was just—"

"You've got dry rot in the back wall, a failing breaker box, and at least one support beam that's out of alignment. Structural issues come first."

She blinked.
"You just walked in. How do you even know that?"

"Been doing this a long time," he said, kneeling to peer under the counter. "It's practically waving at me."

Ava bristled.
"Well, maybe I don't want everything ripped apart on day one. I want this place to feel like my grandmother's bakery again."

Declan paused. His head turned slightly—not enough to be soft, but enough to show he'd heard the word grandmother.

"That your grandma's?" he asked, nodding toward the counter.

Ava followed his gaze—and froze.

Her grandmother's recipe book sat there, worn and soft at the edges, like a living memory. The gold embossing was faded, the spine cracked from decades of flipping. She hadn't realized she'd unpacked it.

A tenderness flickered across Declan's face before he caught it and masked it with a scowl.

Ava picked up the book and held it to her chest.
"She taught me everything in here."

Declan nodded once, unusually quiet.
"Then you should take it home. Safe from dust and falling objects."

Ava blinked at the unexpected gentleness.

But then he stood, business mode snapping back.
"I'll get you a quote."

He pulled a small notebook from his back pocket—lined, beat-up, practical—and scribbled numbers so fast it made Ava's stomach twist.

"How bad?" she asked.

He tore the page out, handed it to her, and she unfolded it slowly.

Her breath stopped.
"That's... that's more than I paid for my car."

"Probably worth more than your car," he said.

Ava stared at the number again.
"No, this can't be right. Are you renovating a palace?"

"Just keeping this place from collapsing on you."

"I can't afford this," Ava whispered. "Not even close."

Declan's expression softened only a fraction.
"You want honest, that's honest. This bakery needs major work."

She swallowed. Hard.
"This is my grandmother's bakery," she said quietly. "I can't just walk away."

"Didn't say you should."

He hooked his tape measure back onto his belt.
"But you asked for a quote. That's the quote."

Ava stared at the paper in her hand, her vision blurring. For a moment, the whole room seemed to tilt—like the bakery itself was holding its breath.

Declan headed for the door, pausing in the frame.
"One more thing," he said, glancing over his shoulder.
"Don't touch anything that looks loose. Especially the ceiling. You've had enough near-death experiences for one morning."

She scowled.
"That was dramatic."

"Not as dramatic as you'll be if the next one actually hits you."

Then he walked out, leaving Ava with dust in her hair, a
recipe book in her hands, and a renovation bill that felt like a
punch to the ribs.

he stared after him.
"Of all the contractors in the world…"
She glared at the ceiling.
"Why'd it have to be that one?"

But something inside her—something stubborn—lifted its
chin.
She wasn't giving up.
Not on the bakery.
Not on her grandmother's legacy.
And definitely not because of one irritatingly handsome man
with sawdust in his hair.

Ava squared her shoulders.
If the bakery wanted to challenge her, fine.

She'd push back.
Just like her grandmother would have wanted.

CHAPTER 4

The dust had barely settled from her morning of clearing debris when Ava heard the bell above the bakery door jingle— smoothly this time, as if someone had actually fixed it before opening it.

Ava frowned.
Declan wasn't due back until tomorrow.

She wiped her hands on her jeans and stepped out from the back room—only to nearly trip over her own feet.

Standing in the center of the bakery was a man who looked like he had stepped out of a city skyline: tailored navy suit, polished shoes, hair styled like he actually used product. He held a leather folder under one arm and wore a smile that was all teeth and no warmth.

"Ava Carson?" he asked, voice smooth as polished marble.

"...Yes?" She straightened instinctively, wishing she didn't have plaster dust smudged across her cheek.

He extended a perfectly manicured hand.
"Evan Rourke. Rourke Development Group."

Ava blinked.
"The... what group?"

"Rourke Development. We specialize in revitalizing underutilized properties in small towns."

He gestured around the bakery with a sympathetic, prepackaged smile.
"Properties like this one."

Ava's stomach tightened.
"Revitalizing how?"

"Well," he said lightly, "we bring in recognizable brands, modernize the storefronts, increase foot traffic, improve tax revenue—"

"You mean chain cafés."
She crossed her arms.
"You want to put one in here."

Evan's smile didn't falter. If anything, it brightened.
"Maple Ridge is the perfect town for expansion. And this building? Excellent location."

He took a step closer, lowering his voice as if they were old friends sharing a secret.
"I heard you inherited this place unexpectedly. Must be overwhelming."

It was said gently... but it landed with the weight of a brick.
Ava swallowed.
"I'm managing."

"Of course you are."
He tilted his head, studying the cracked tile on the floor, the exposed beam overhead, the dust still drifting lazily in the air.
"But managing and thriving are two different things."

Ava's pulse ticked faster.
"What are you really here for?"

Evan finally opened the folder.
Inside was a contract. Glossy pages. Blue sticky notes marking signature lines.
"We want to buy the property," he said.
"Quick closing. Cash offer. No inspections required."

Ava's breath stopped.
Cash.
Fast cash.
A way out.

An escape hatch from crumbling ceilings and impossible renovation costs and running into Declan and Elias like she'd never actually left this town.

She forced her voice steady.
"Why now? Why so fast?"

"Because someone else will grab it if we don't."
He smiled like that was meant to reassure her.
"And because this place is... well. Let's just say it's time for something new."

Ava felt heat crawl up her neck.
Something about the way he said "this place" made her chest tighten.

"It's my grandmother's bakery," she said quietly.

He nodded sympathetically—too sympathetically.
"I understand sentimental value. Truly. But sentiment doesn't fix structural rot."

Ava flinched as if he'd physically struck the bakery.

Evan continued, flipping to the last page of the contract.
"You'd walk away with enough to start fresh anywhere you want. No debt. No stress. No collapsing ceilings."
His eyes softened.
"You don't have to do this the hard way, Ava."

Her heart thudded painfully.
For a second—just one—she imagined it.
Leaving the mess behind.
Leaving the fear.
Leaving the past.

She imagined walking away with money in her pocket instead of splinters in her hands.
She imagined freedom.
But then... she looked around the bakery.
At the faded yellow paint.
At the sticker on the pastry case.
At the recipe book on the shelf, tucked safely out of harm's way.
Her grandmother's handwriting echoed through her memory:
Make something that brings people joy, sweetheart.
A chain café wasn't joy.
It was convenience.
It was noise.

It was the exact opposite of everything her grandmother had taught her.

Ava lifted her chin.
"No."

Evan blinked.
"...Pardon?"

"No," she repeated, firmer. "I'm not selling."

Something cold flickered behind his polite expression.
"Ava... be reasonable."

"I am."
Her voice didn't shake this time.
"This bakery stays mine."

Evan held her gaze for a long beat—too long.
Then he smiled again, but the charm was gone.
Replaced by calculation.
"Well," he said softly, sliding the contract back into his folder,
"if you change your mind... you won't have much time."
Ava frowned.

"What does that mean?"

But he was already walking toward the door.
He paused with one hand on the frame.
"Buildings like this? They don't last forever. Neither does opportunity."

The bell chimed sharply as he left.
Silence filled the bakery again—but this time it pulsed with tension.
Ava pressed her hand to her chest, feeling her heartbeat race.
She had refused him.
She had chosen the bakery—chosen her grandmother—chosen the hard road.
She just wished it didn't terrify her quite so much.

CHAPTER 5

Ava stared at her phone for a good thirty seconds before finally pressing Call.
Her stomach twisted as it rang—once, twice, three times—Declan answered with his usual charm.

"What broke now?"

Ava blinked. "Nothing broke. Yet."

"That's surprising."

She closed her eyes and exhaled.
"Declan, I need to talk to you. About the estimate."

There was a short pause. Not cold—just cautious.
"You ready to abandon ship?" he asked.

"No," she said quickly. "Actually... I want to hire you."
Another pause—this one longer.

"Say that again? My reception must've cut out."
She rolled her eyes. "I said I want to hire you."

"Well, that's unexpected."

"Why?"

"Because you looked like you were going to faint when you saw the numbers."

"I still feel like I might faint," she admitted. "But after the day I had, I realized something—I have to do this. I'm not letting some developer turn this place into a brick-and-marble coffee empire."

Declan let out a breath that sounded almost like approval. "Alright. Then let's talk."

Ava met him at the bakery ten minutes later.
Declan stepped inside carrying a clipboard and a coffee, both
of which seemed permanently attached to him. He surveyed
the room like he was assessing a crime scene.

"So," he said, flipping to a new page, "what's your budget?"

Ava winced. "I don't really have a number yet."

"That's not comforting."

"Declan, I want to do this right. I just can't do it all at once."

He softened—barely, but enough to notice.
"We'll prioritize the structural issues," he said. "Beam
replacement first, then electrical. Everything cosmetic waits."

She nodded. "Okay."

"And I'll shuffle some jobs around," he added. "Try to get you
on-site sooner."

Ava blinked. "Really?"

"Don't get emotional about it," he murmured, scribbling on
the clipboard. "It's just scheduling."

"It's still really nice of you."

He made a noncommittal sound, then stepped closer.
"You've got flour on your cheek."

Her breath hitched.
"What—really?" She lifted her hand to wipe it.

Declan stopped her with one finger raised.
"No, you'll smudge it."
He reached forward—slowly, attentively—and brushed the bit
of flour away with his thumb.

A spark flared, bright and surprising.
Ava swallowed. Hard.
"Thanks."

Declan didn't move for a heartbeat.
"You're welcome."
Then he stepped back and cleared his throat, snapping the comfortable tension in half.
"Alright. Day one of demo starts tomorrow."

"Tomorrow? That fast?"

"You wanted ASAP, didn't you?"

She smiled despite the chaos swirling inside her.
"Yeah. I did."
...
Construction day came with the smell of sawdust and the sound of hammering echoing through the old bakery. Declan worked with laser focus, removing damaged boards, reinforcing beams, and muttering about whoever last remodeled the place being "a menace to humanity."
Ava hovered nearby, sweeping debris, fetching tools, and trying to stay out of his way. Every so often, she caught him glancing at her—quick, subtle looks he pretended weren't happening.
And every so often, she caught herself doing the same.
By late afternoon, the air buzzed with progress... and the faint possibility of something new growing between them.

Ava stepped outside to toss a bag of debris, savoring the cool breeze—
—and froze.
Elias was walking down the sidewalk toward her.

He stopped when their eyes met.
"Ava," he said, breathless like he'd hurried. "I've been trying to catch you."

She straightened.
"What's going on?"

"I heard about yesterday. The ceiling... Declan being here..."
His gaze flicked past her toward the bakery. Something tightened in his jaw. "Is he working for you now?"

"Yes," she said carefully. "I hired him."

Elias took a slow breath. "Ava, look... I know we didn't end things the best way—"

"That's an understatement."

He winced. "I deserved that. But I want to help."

She blinked. "Help? How?"
"I know people. Electricians, local suppliers, inspectors. I can get you deals. Favors. Whatever you need."

He stepped closer. "I want to make things right between us. I never stopped—"

"Ava?" Declan called from inside. "You good out there?"

Elias's expression darkened, jealousy flickering like a struck match.

Ava stood between their voices, their histories, their tension. Two men from her past and present—one steady, one stormy— colliding like they had every intention of complicating her life.

She exhaled slowly.
"I appreciate the offer, Elias," she said. "But I need to figure this out myself."

His shoulders dropped.
"Right. Okay. But... I'm not giving up."
He walked away, glancing back twice.

Ava looked toward the bakery, where the sound of Declan's hammer echoed through the open door.
Just what she needed.
Two men. Old wounds. New sparks.
And a bakery ready to crush her and her heart if she wasn't careful.

She rubbed her temples and groaned.
"This is going to get messy," she whispered.

Declan leaned out the doorway.
"What's going to get messy?"

"Nothing," she said too quickly.

He raised one brow. "Uh-huh."

Ava forced a smile she didn't feel.
Tomorrow, she'd deal with the bakery.
And Declan.
And Elias.
But tonight?
She was going to lie down...
and pray the ceiling didn't fall again.

CHAPTER 6

The first time the water line burst, it sounded like the bakery was swallowing itself.
Ava was in the front, rearranging the chalkboard menu for the third time that morning—still no customers, still no pastries, just hopeful handwriting—when a violent hiss split the air, followed by a heavy gushing thud from the kitchen.

She dropped the chalk.
"Declan?" she called. "What was that?"

His answer was drowned out by the unmistakable sound of water going exactly where it shouldn't.

"Oh no," Ava whispered, and ran.
She barreled through the swinging door into the kitchen—and skidded to a stop.

Water sprayed in a wild arc from a copper pipe near the back wall, slamming into a stack of empty crates and ricocheting across the floor. A shallow lake was already forming, curling around table legs and creeping toward the big mixer like it was planning a coup.

Declan stood in the middle of it, jeans soaked to mid-calf, one hand braced on the pipe, the other reaching for a wrench on the floor.

"What happened?" she yelped, splashing toward him.

He didn't look up. "Pipe decided it's retired."

"This isn't funny!"

"Didn't say it was."
Another burst of water hit his shoulder. He grimaced, tightening his grip.

"Ava, I need you to move those crates and grab me the shut-off valve handle from the toolbox."

She blinked. "The what from the what?"

"Red handle. Metal toolbox. By the back door. Go."

There was something in his voice—steady, sharp—that cut through her panic. She ran for the toolbox, nearly slipping, and flipped the latches with shaking hands.
Red handle, red handle...
There. She grabbed it and hurried back, the hem of her jeans soaking instantly as she stepped into the spreading water.

"Here," she said, thrusting it toward him.
He took it, their fingers brushing for half a second—warm, calloused, grounding.

"Good. Now go to the back corner." He nodded behind her. "You'll see a valve low on the wall. Fit this on and turn it clockwise. Hard."

She spun around, heart pounding. The valve was half-hidden behind an old flour sack, already damp. She shoved the sack aside, jammed the handle on, and turned.
It didn't budge.
"Declan!" she called. "It's stuck!"

"Use both hands," he said. "And your whole stubborn personality."

She would've laughed if she wasn't busy imagining the bakery drifting away like a houseboat.
Ava gritted her teeth, planted her feet in the cold water, and twisted with everything she had.
The valve groaned—then gave.
The spray weakened, sputtered, and finally narrowed to an angry trickle.

Declan let out a relieved breath and stepped back, running a hand through his dripping hair. "There we go."

Ava leaned against the wall, breathing hard. "Is... is it over?"

"For now." He gave the pipe a final glare, as if daring it to misbehave again. "You okay?"

She looked down at herself. Her shirt was splattered. Her jeans were soaked. Her socks squished.
"No," she said. "But thanks for asking."

For a second, his mouth twitched.
"There's a mop in the closet."

She groaned. "Of course there is."
He moved past her to grab a bucket, his shoulder brushing hers. Even after being sprayed by half the town's water supply, he somehow managed to look solid. Unshaken.

"You weren't kidding," she said, scanning the puddle. "This place really is trying to kill me."

"I warned you." He shrugged. "Old buildings always throw a tantrum before they cooperate."
"Like toddlers."
"Worse. These leak."
She huffed out a helpless little laugh, surprised to hear it echo off the damp walls.

Declan glanced at her, a faint smile finally breaking through. "There it is."

"There what is?"

"The part of you that laughs instead of spiraling."

"I don't spiral."

He looked pointedly at the floor, the pipe, and the still-dripping crates.

She sighed. "Okay, I spiral a little."

"A little," he agreed. "But you also turned a stubborn valve that most people twice your size wouldn't touch."

A warm flush crept up her neck. "Adrenaline. And the fear of drowning in my own bakery."

"Whatever works."

They worked in companionable silence for the next fifteen minutes—mopping, pushing water toward the floor drain, moving crates to drier territory. Every so often, their eyes met and darted away again, like both of them were a little surprised to be... almost getting along.

When the worst of the mess was gone, Ava tossed the soaked mop back into the bucket and brushed damp hair from her face.
"I'm making coffee," she declared. "And something with sugar. For my nerves."

"You don't have running water in the front," Declan reminded her.

"Who said I was using the sink?" She nodded toward the stack of bottled water she'd brought in for just such emergencies. "I came vaguely prepared."

He huffed a quiet sound that was almost definitely a laugh. "Knock yourself out."

She hesitated. "You want some?"

"You're the one almost drowning."

"You were in here too," she countered.

He looked at her for a long second. "Yeah. Coffee would be good."

Something eased in her chest. "Okay. Don't let the pipe explode again while I'm gone."

"I'll do my best."

...

Twenty minutes later, the front of the bakery smelled faintly like her grandmother's kitchen.

Ava stood at the makeshift counter she'd set up with a hot plate and a portable oven, watching the cinnamon rolls rise. She'd had to improvise the pans and the proofing time, but muscle memory guided her hands almost as much as the faded lines in her grandmother's notebook.

She shouldn't be baking when half the kitchen was torn apart. She shouldn't be using precious ingredients before the bakery even officially reopened.

But after the pipe incident, she needed the ritual.
She needed comfort.
And maybe, just maybe, she wanted to see what happened when Declan Hayes took a bite of a proper Buttered Biscuit cinnamon roll.

When the timer chimed, she pulled the tray out carefully. The rolls were golden, their spirals of cinnamon sugar bubbling at the edges, icing ready in a chipped mixing bowl beside her.

Ava smiled, her heart giving a strange little twist. "Okay, Grandma," she murmured. "Let's see if the magic still works."

She iced them one by one, steam curling up into her face, smelling like every Saturday morning of her childhood. When she was satisfied, she arranged four on a plate and carried them to the kitchen.

Declan was on a ladder when she walked in, examining the pipe and murmuring something distinctly unflattering under his breath.

"Truce offering," Ava called. "In pastry form."

He looked down, brows lifting. "What is that?"

"You've never seen a cinnamon roll before?"

"Not one that looks like that." He climbed down, wiping his hands on a rag. "Smells like a sugar bomb."

"That's the point."
He hesitated, glancing between her and the plate. "You don't

have to feed me, you know. You're already paying me."

"This isn't about owing you," she said. "You saved my floor from becoming an indoor pool. Let me say thank you."

Something flickered across his face—something almost like discomfort.
Slowly, he took one.
The moment his fingers sank into the soft dough, his expression changed. He stared at it like it had just said something in a language only he understood.

Ava tilted her head. "You okay?"

He didn't answer. He brought it to his mouth and took a bite.
His eyes closed.
Just for a second. Just long enough for her to see it.
The tension in his shoulders loosened. His jaw unclenched. He looked suddenly, painfully... young.
Then he swallowed, opened his eyes, and shoved the reaction behind a familiar wall of gruffness.

"It's fine," he said.

"Fine?" she repeated. "That sounded like more than fine."

"Decent," he amended. "For a sugar bomb."

Ava narrowed her eyes. "You're a terrible liar."

He took another bite. A bigger one.

She crossed her arms. "You're not getting more until you admit it's good."

He chewed, gaze dropping to the plate. When he finally looked up, there was something raw in his expression she hadn't seen before.

"My mom used to make these," he said quietly. "Every Sunday."

Her chest tightened. "I didn't know."

"Not your fault."

"What happened?" she asked gently.

He hesitated. His thumb brushed a smudge of icing on his palm, like he needed something to do with his hands.
"She got sick," he said. "A long time ago. After she died, my dad... stopped caring about that kind of thing. I think I just decided it hurt less to pretend I didn't, either."

Ava's throat closed up for a moment.
"I'm sorry," she whispered.

He shrugged, but it was the kind of shrug that hurt to watch.
"It was a long time ago."

Silence settled between them, softer this time. Thick with sugar and something bittersweet.

She nudged the plate toward him. "Have another."
He hesitated.
"It's not pretending," she said. "If something makes you feel... good."

His gaze searched hers, like he was testing whether or not she would flinch at the weight of his answer.
Then he picked up a second roll.

"I'll deduct this from your invoice," he said.

She laughed, startled. "You absolutely will not."

"Labor cost," he insisted.

"You're impossible."

"And you're bossy."

They smiled at each other then, really smiled, for the first time since he'd walked into her collapsing bakery.
The moment was interrupted by a sharp knock from the front.
Ava jumped. "We're not open yet!"
The knock came again, followed by a too-familiar voice calling,

"Ava? You in there?"

Elias.
Of course.

Declan's brow furrowed. "You expecting someone?"

"Unfortunately." She set the plate down and wiped her hands on a towel, suddenly aware of the flour smudge on her cheek and the fact that Declan was still standing a little too close.

"Friend of yours?" he asked.

"Something like that," she said. "You should... probably keep doing whatever you were doing. He doesn't need to know how close this place came to becoming an aquarium."

"Sure," Declan said, but his gaze flicked toward the front with a spark of curiosity.

As she headed out of the kitchen, Ava felt the weight of two different histories pressing on her—the unresolved past with Elias, and the unexpected softness cracking open inside her around Declan.

For the first time, the bakery didn't feel like just a building she had to save.
It felt like a crossroads.
And she had no idea which way her heart would go.

CHAPTER 7

Maple Ridge always looked prettiest in late afternoon.

The sunlight fell in soft gold across the storefronts, catching on windows and old brick and the hand-painted signs her grandmother used to praise on every walk. Ava hadn't meant to wander, but after a morning of construction noise and a minor argument with a stubborn water valve, she needed air.
She took a slow breath.

The town felt... warmer than she remembered. Like it had been holding its breath, waiting for her to come home.
Mrs. Dunlop from the quilting shop spotted her first.

"Ava Carson?" she gasped, clasping her hands. "Oh honey, look at you! You're the spitting image of your grandmother."
Ava smiled, surprised at how good it felt. "Hi, Mrs. Dunlop. It's good to see you."

"Your grandma would be over the moon you're fixing that bakery. We've all missed the smell of her croissants drifting down Main Street." Her eyes softened. "You bring that back, you hear?"

Ava swallowed. "I'm trying."

She heard the warmth behind every greeting she received after that—shop owners waving, an elderly couple asking about renovation progress, kids racing by on scooters shouting, "Are you the bakery lady?"

She laughed. "Not yet!"
But for the first time since returning, she believed she could be.
...

As the sunlight dipped lower, her steps carried her to the quiet edge of town almost on instinct. The cemetery gate

creaked open as she pushed it. She'd avoided coming here her
first few days home. Too raw. Too final.
But today felt... right.
She followed the familiar path to the maple tree—the one her
grandmother always said had the best shade on earth. The
headstone sat beneath it, simple and elegant.

Margaret Carson
Beloved Baker, Beloved Heart

Ava knelt, brushing leaves away with her hand.
"Hi, Grandma," she whispered. "I don't know if I'm doing any
of this right. I'm probably not. The roof tried to kill me. Twice.
Declan keeps telling me everything is about to collapse. And I
think the oven hates me."

Her voice cracked softly.
"But I'm trying. I love this place. I love what you built. I just...
hope I'm worthy of carrying it."
She blinked tears away before they could fall.

A soft crunch sounded behind her.
She stiffened and turned—
Declan.
He stood a few feet away, hands in his pockets, expression
unreadable but gentler than usual. His hair was dusted with
sawdust, still in his work clothes, like he had come straight
from the bakery.
"I didn't mean to interrupt," he said quietly.

She rose slowly. "It's okay. What... what are you doing here?"

Declan hesitated, eyes shifting to the headstone.
"I come here sometimes," he admitted. "Your grandmother...
she was kind to me. Kinder than most adults when I was a kid."

Ava's breath stilled. "You knew her?"

He nodded once, jaw tightening—not with anger, with
emotion he wasn't sure he should show.
"She used to give me the messed-up pastries," he said. "The
ones that didn't come out perfect. Said every kid deserved
something sweet. Especially the ones life had roughed up a

bit."

Ava felt her chest warm painfully.
"She never told me that."

"Didn't want credit," Declan murmured. "She just... cared."

Silence settled between them, soft and full.

Ava stepped closer—just a little—and Declan didn't move away.
"I'm glad you came," she whispered.
He finally met her eyes. Something flickered there—a quiet longing he didn't have words for.

"You looked like you needed someone," he said.
His voice was low, roughened with sincerity.

Ava's heart thudded.
"I did," she admitted.

A gentle breeze stirred her hair. Declan reached up instinctively—then paused, his fingers hovering near her cheek, asking permission without a word.

Ava didn't pull away.

His fingertips brushed a loose strand back behind her ear. The touch was careful... almost reverent. His hand lingered a second longer than needed, warm against her cheek.
Declan swallowed, looking at her like she was something fragile and fierce all at once.

"I don't want to make things complicated for you," he said, voice barely above a whisper.

"You already have," she breathed.
A faint, helpless smile tugged at his mouth.

His thoughts were written in his eyes:
She's trouble.
She's hope.
She's everything I should stay away from.
But I don't want to.

He stepped back slightly—not to retreat, but to steady himself.

"I should get back," he said softly. "That beam itself."

Ava nodded, trying to gather air back into her lungs. "Declan?"

He looked over his shoulder.

"Thank you," she said. "For being here."

His gaze softened like melting amber. "Anytime."

And she knew he meant it.

CHAPTER 8

By the time the sun dipped below the ridge of old brick buildings, the bakery looked half-reborn and half-wrecked. The walls were patched but unpainted, the lighting half-installed, the smell of sawdust mixing strangely with lingering sugar from past decades.

Ava wiped her forehead with the back of her wrist and glanced across the room.

Declan was still working.
He knelt near the new support beam, adjusting clamps, the lamplight casting warm amber across his shoulders. His T-shirt was faded and flecked with wood dust, clinging in all the ways she tried—and failed—not to stare at.

"You know," Ava said, leaning against the counter, "normal people stop working when it gets dark."

Declan didn't look up. "Good thing neither of us is normal."

A smile tugged at her mouth. "Speak for yourself."

"I am," he said. "I'm a mess."

She laughed softly, surprised by it. A month ago, he would've said something abrupt or sarcastic or painfully literal. Now there was a softness tucked into the edges of his voice, like he'd finally stopped holding his breath around her.

He tightened one last bolt and stood, wiping his hands on his jeans.
"There." He nodded at the beam. "Solid as it gets."

Ava wandered closer. "You make it look easy."

"It's not." His eyes flicked to hers. "But doing it for you... I don't mind."

Her heart stuttered.
She looked away, suddenly very interested in the floor. "I made coffee."

"That why you're jittery?" he teased.

"Maybe I just have a low tolerance for caffeine."

"Or me."
She blinked at him. Declan rarely flirted—at least not on purpose.

She held out a mug. "Here. Before your jokes get worse."
He took it, their fingers brushing—just barely, just enough.
And it jolted through her like warm sugar.

Declan froze for half a second. One breath. Two.
Then he cleared his throat and pretended to examine the mug.
"It's good," he said after a sip.

"It's terrible," she laughed. "I used the emergency generic stuff."

Declan winced. "I was trying to be polite."

"You? Polite?" She gave him a mock gasp. "Should I call the press?"

He shook his head, but a faint smile pulled at his cheek. A real one. Not the guarded smirk he used as armor.
They drank in comfortable silence for a moment.
Ava walked toward the front windows, staring out at Maple Ridge's empty main street. The streetlamps glowed amber. A soft fog curled at the edges of the sidewalks. The whole town breathed quietly.

"Feels strange being back," Ava said, her voice soft. "Like everything is familiar but... different. Like the world kept going without me."

Declan stepped up beside her—not close enough to crowd her, not far enough to feel detached. Just... near. A warm presence.

Hours passed in easy rhythm.
Measure. Cut. Laugh. Glance. Look away too late.
At one point Ava lost her grip on the trim board and nearly
knocked over a bucket of nails.

Declan caught it—then her elbow. "I know the feeling," he
said quietly.

Ava looked up at him. "Yeah?"

Declan's jaw tightened. "Yeah."

It wasn't a conversation he was ready for—not yet. But
something in the way he said it made her chest tighten.
"So what brought you here?" she asked gently. "To Maple
Ridge."

Declan hesitated. His thumb brushed the rim of his coffee
mug. "Needed a change."

"That's the short version."

He smirked faintly. "It's the only version tonight."

Ava nudged him with her elbow. "Fine. But one day you're
telling me the long one."

"Maybe," he said, eyes softening. "If you stick around long
enough."

A slow heat unfurled beneath her ribs.
For a moment, the only sound was the hum of the lamplight
and the faint buzz of night insects outside.

Ava set her mug down. "Want help with that trim board?"

Declan blinked. "You want to help with power tools?"

"I'm a brave woman."

"You're holding the hammer backwards."

She looked down. "...I knew that."

He chuckled—a low, warm sound she hadn't heard before. "Come here."

He stepped behind her, guiding her hands gently. His palms hovered over hers, close enough to share breath, close enough to feel the heat of him along her spine.

"Hold it like this," he murmured.

Her pulse jumped.

He paused, noticing—but he didn't pull away. Not immediately.

When he finally stepped back, Ava felt the cold of his absence like a draft.
"So," he said, clearing his throat, "you're pretty good at this."

"Pretty good?"

"Okay, terrible."
A grin.

"But enthusiastic."
She laughed—bright, warm, unfiltered.

"You okay?" he asked, voice low.

"Fine," she whispered, suddenly aware of how close they stood. Their arms grazed, their breaths mixing in the warm sawdust-thick air.

His eyes flicked to her lips—brief, unintentional, charged. He looked away first.
"We should call it a night," he said roughly.

"Probably," she whispered.
But neither of them moved.

Finally, Declan stepped back, running a hand through his hair. "Same time tomorrow?"

"Yeah." Ava smiled softly. "Same time."

He walked to the door, pausing before stepping out into the quiet night.
"Ava," he said without turning around.

"Yes?"

"You're doing good work here."
He said it gently. Intimately. Like he meant more than the bakery.
Then he left.

Ava stood in the middle of the half-finished bakery, heart fluttering wildly, unable to stop smiling.

Something was changing.
Something was warming.
Something was beginning.
And she wasn't sure if she was ready.
But she hoped she was.

CHAPTER 9

By late morning, the bakery smelled faintly of sawdust, fresh coffee, and something else Ava was starting to associate with Declan Hayes—quiet competence wrapped in trouble. He worked with his usual intensity, focused on reinforcing the back wall while Ava reorganized a stack of supplies.

She kept stealing glances at him.
Not obvious ones.
Just... little looks.
The way his shoulders moved when he lifted a beam.
The way he brushed sawdust from his hair.
The way he sometimes smiled—barely—when she made a snarky comment.

It felt like something had shifted between them.
She didn't know what yet.
But it was there.

Ava stepped outside to take a quick break, breathing the crisp Maple Ridge air. The town was waking up; shops were opening, locals waved, and the coffee shop across the street released its morning crowd.

She was about to head back in when she heard it.
Two voices.
Low, hushed, just around the corner of the building.

"—I'm telling you, Declan Hayes is trouble," an older woman whispered. Ava recognized her voice—Marcy Leland, queen of Maple Ridge gossip.

"Oh, come on," another replied. "Trouble how?"

"You didn't hear about his divorce?"

Ava froze.
She didn't want to listen... but the words pulled her in anyway.

"Messy as they come," Marcy said. "Wife walked out, left him the house, the dog, and a mountain of debt."

"That doesn't sound messy. That sounds sad."

"Oh, it gets better." Marcy sniffed sharply, like even remembering the story offended her. "He lost a business deal. Something big. Folks say it ruined him for a while. After that? He stopped letting people in. Stoic as a stone wall."

The second woman paused.
"...Think he's still carrying it?"

"Still carrying it? Honey, he walks around with ghosts."

Ava's stomach tightened.
She should stop listening.
This wasn't fair to him.
But now the whispers came out faster—like they'd been waiting years for an audience.

"I swear, that man doesn't want to be happy," Marcy said. "He keeps to himself. Never dates. Never smiles. If he's working with that Carson girl, she better keep her distance."

Ava bristled at that.

"I've met Ava," the second woman said. "She's sweet. And she's got a good head on her shoulders."

"Well, she'll need it. Declan's the type who'll break your heart without meaning to. Not because he's cruel, but because he's still living in whatever disaster came before."

Footsteps shifted. The women moved on.
Ava stayed perfectly still.
The words settled over her like dust—unwanted, irritating, impossible to ignore.
She didn't believe in gossip.
She hated gossip.
But the town's whispers burrowed under her skin anyway.
A failed marriage.
A business collapse.

A man carrying ghosts.

Slowly, she turned back toward the bakery door.

Declan stood inside, bent over a support beam, sleeves pushed up, jaw set in that stubborn way of his.

Something in Ava ached unexpectedly.
Was he really carrying that much pain?
And if he was...
Why did she want to understand it?

She stepped back inside, forcing her heartbeat to steady.

Declan didn't look up. "Everything okay?"

Ava swallowed. "Yeah. Fine. Just getting some fresh air."
He paused mid-measurement, eyes lifting to hers—dark, warm, unreadable.

"You sure?"
There was something in his voice.
A flicker of concern.
A softness he rarely let show.

Ava nodded too quickly.
"Yep. Totally fine."

But as she watched him return to his work, focused and quiet and impossibly guarded, one thought refused to loosen its grip: There's so much more to him than he lets anyone see.

And whether she wanted to or not, Ava Carson was already falling into the gravity of Declan Hayes's untold story.

CHAPTER 10

Saturday morning arrived with the kind of crisp, sunny air that made Maple Ridge feel like a postcard. Ava balanced two trays of sample pastries against her hip as she navigated the crowded farmer's market—cinnamon twists on one tray, mini berry turnovers on the other.

This was her first public step toward rebuilding the bakery's reputation, and nerves fluttered inside her like trapped birds. Her grandmother used to say, If the people taste your heart, they'll come back for more.

Ava hoped to God that was true.
She reached the small wooden booth a volunteer had saved for her. A handwritten sign read:
The Buttered Biscuit — Coming Back Soon!

A few locals recognized her immediately.

"Ava Carson? Well I'll be!"

"Your grandmother would be so proud."

"You're reopening the bakery? Oh, we've missed it!"

Their enthusiasm warmed her like sunlight. She set out the samples, smoothing the tablecloth, arranging the treats just so. She tried to ignore how badly her hands were shaking.
Please taste good. Please not be terrible. Please—

"Looks good."

Ava jumped.
Declan stood a few feet away, hands in his pockets, looking infuriatingly casual. Cargo pants. Gray T-shirt. Aviators he absolutely did not need in the shade. He pretended to be inspecting apples at the neighboring booth, but the smirk

tugging at his mouth gave him away.

"You're early," Ava said, crossing her arms. "And pretending to shop for produce."

"I needed carrots," he replied, holding up a bunch. He lowered his sunglasses. "Totally believable."

She snorted. "You came to check on me."

"No," he said. Then added, "Maybe."

Before she could tease him, a kid barreled through the crowd, chasing a runaway balloon.
"Ava, watch—"

Declan moved fast. His hand came to Ava's waist, steadying her as the kid slammed into his side instead of her tray.
The pastries wobbled but held.
Ava stared up at Declan, breath caught.
His hand stayed on her just a beat too long. Warm. Solid. Protective.

"You okay?" he asked softly.

"Yes," she whispered. "Thanks."

He cleared his throat and stepped back like the moment had surprised him too.
The older couple running the honey booth grinned knowingly.
Ava pretended not to notice.
...

The morning flowed smoothly after that. People sampled her pastries and gave feedback:
"Just like your grandmother's!"
"Are you taking preorders?"
"When are you reopening?"

Each comment lightened something inside her.
Declan hovered but tried not to. He circled the booths. Talked to the jam lady. Pretended to examine pumpkins. But every few minutes, his gaze flicked back to her.

At one point, she caught him smiling—a real one, soft and unguarded—when he thought she wasn't looking.
A warmth spread through her chest.
After the rush slowed, Ava took a breath and leaned against the booth.

Declan returned, holding two steaming paper cups.
"Coffee?" he said, offering one. "From the guy down the row. It's not yours, but... good enough."

She took the cup, brushing his fingers in the exchange.
The touch jolted her—not electric exactly, but warm, like a match striking.
"Thanks," she murmured.

He nodded at her display. "You did good today."

"You sound surprised."

"Not surprised," he said. "Just... proud."

The word hung between them.
Ava's heart thudded once, hard.

Declan looked away first, swallowing, as if the honesty had slipped out before he could catch it.

The volunteer at the next booth leaned over.
"Adorable. You two need a booth together."

Ava nearly dropped her coffee.
Declan choked on his.

...

As they packed up, the sun warm on their backs, Ava felt lighter than she had in months. The market's energy, Declan's presence, the sense that people actually wanted the bakery back—it all filled her with something unfamiliar. Hope.

Declan carried the heavier tray without asking. "Let me walk you to your car."

"You don't have to—"

"I know."
He said it gently.

When they reached her trunk, she hesitated.

Declan noticed, leaning one hand on the car as he studied her.
"What?"

"Nothing," she said. "Just... thank you. For today."

"It was nothing."

"It wasn't."

Their eyes held.
For a moment—just a moment—the noise of the market dimmed, and the world seemed to tilt toward him.
He felt it too. She could see it in the way his breath caught, the way his eyes softened, the way he didn't step back.
But he did eventually.

"See you tomorrow," he said quietly, turning.

"Yeah," Ava whispered. "Tomorrow."

She watched him go, feeling something inside her shift.
Something deep.
Something dangerous.
Something wonderful.

CHAPTER 11

The storm rolled in fast.

One moment the sky over Maple Ridge was a pastel watercolor—soft pinks, gentle gold—
and the next, clouds thickened like wet charcoal, swallowing the light.

Ava barely had time to stack the last clean tray behind the bakery counter before the power flickered once... twice... Then everything went black.

"Of course," she whispered into the darkness. "Perfect timing."
The air hummed with silence—no refrigerators, no overhead lights, no buzzing neon sign outside. Just the storm wind pressing against the windows like an impatient guest.
She fumbled for her phone's flashlight, knocking into a mixing bowl in the dark.

A low voice spoke from behind her, warm and steady.
"You okay?"

Ava spun, lifting the tiny beam, and nearly collided with Declan.
He stood in the doorway dripping rain, shirt damp, hair tousled, looking like he'd walked straight out of the storm just to find her.

"Declan? What are you doing here?"

"Power's out everywhere." He shrugged, stepping inside. "Figured you might need a hand."

A flutter moved through her chest—annoyingly strong, annoyingly warm.
"I'm fine," she said. "Just cleaning up."

"You can't see anything."

"I was managing."

He raised a brow. "You just elbowed a bowl onto the floor."

"It was already crooked," she lied.

A faint, barely-there smile tugged at his mouth. "Sure it was."

Another sharp wind gust rattled the windows. The bakery felt suddenly smaller, lit only by the soft glow of Ava's phone.

"Here," Declan said quietly. "Let me get candles."

"You know where they are?"

"Found them yesterday. You reorganize nothing."

Ava huffed. "This is how my grandmother stored things."
"And she was five feet tall and didn't lift lumber."

He disappeared into the back. A moment later, warm candlelight bloomed, casting golden halos across the walls and soft shadows over Declan's face.

Ava felt something in her loosen.
"Thanks," she murmured.

Declan nodded, wiping rain from his hair. "Storm's pretty bad. Roads are flooding a little already."

Her stomach tightened. "Do you need to head home?"

He hesitated. "Not if you need help here."

The way he said it—quiet, certain—made her chest feel unsteady.
"Actually..." she swallowed, "some of the dough stuck to the counter, and I can't see well enough to scrape it."

Declan grabbed a towel, stepping beside her. Close. Too close.

His arm brushed hers, just lightly, and she felt the warmth of it echo up her skin.

They worked in silence for a moment—his steady presence grounding her in the flickering light.

Then Ava exhaled, long and shaky.
"This whole thing... I don't know what I'm doing," she whispered. "This bakery. Coming home. Everyone thinking I can just... fix everything."

Declan paused, his hand resting on the counter.
"You're doing better than you think."

She shook her head, emotion tightening her throat. "No. My last job burned me out. My ex made me feel like I wasn't enough. And now this place is falling apart just like I am."

Declan turned to her slowly.
The candlelight carved soft gold along his jaw, catching the quiet worry in his eyes.

"Ava," he said, low and rough, "you are not falling apart."
She met his gaze—and the world outside the bakery seemed to disappear.

"You don't even know me," she whispered.

He swallowed. Hard.
"I know enough," he murmured. "I know you walked into a disaster and didn't run. I know you work harder than anyone I've met. And I know..."
His voice caught—barely noticeable, unless someone was standing close enough to feel the breath of it.
"I know you care. Too much, maybe. But that's not a weakness."

A tremor moved through her.
"What about you?" she asked softly. "Everyone has a past. Something that scares them."

Declan's jaw tightened.
For a second—just a second—something raw flickered behind his eyes. Pain. Loss. Words he wasn't ready to speak.
He looked away, wiping a streak of dough from the counter

with exaggerated focus.

"My past doesn't matter," he said quietly.

"But it does," Ava whispered. "To me."

His hands stilled.
And though he didn't say anything, the silence between them
shifted—deeper, heavier, charged with something electric and
tender and dangerous.

A candle crackled softly.

Declan finally looked at her again, and the emotion in his eyes
made her breath hitch.
"Ava," he said, voice low, "some things are better left in the
dark."

She stepped closer—close enough to see the fine rain
droplets still clinging to his shirt.
"Then why don't you ever walk away from me?" she asked.

His breath faltered.
He didn't answer.
He didn't need to.
The tension spoke for him.

Another gust of wind shook the windows, but neither of them
looked away from the other.

Finally, Declan straightened, clearing his throat.
"Let me finish this side of the counter," he said, voice strained.
"You take that part."

Ava nodded, heart pounding, and they worked in silence—
though nothing about the silence felt simple anymore.

When the candles flickered lower, Declan stepped back.
"Storm's easing," he said. "Lights should be back by morning."

"Thanks for staying," she said softly.

He paused at the doorway, hand on the frame.

"I didn't stay because of the storm."

Their eyes met.

And then he left—quiet as he'd arrived—leaving Ava alone in the soft candlelight, wishing she understood him, and terrified that she already did.

CHAPTER 12

The morning light slanted across the bakery floor in warm stripes, catching dust motes drifting lazily through the air. Ava stretched, sore from another late-night sanding session with Declan, and reached for a stack of paint samples.

She didn't hear the door open.
"Ava Carson," a smooth voice said, far too polished for eight a.m.

Ava's stomach tightened. She turned.

Evan Rourke stepped inside wearing a tailored charcoal coat, expensive shoes, and a smile that looked like it cost extra. His presence instantly felt out of place in the dusty, half-gutted bakery.

"Long time no see," he said, as if they'd parted on friendly terms.

She crossed her arms. "You were here three days ago."

"And here I am again." His eyes swept the construction mess with a theatrical wince. "The place is... still standing. Impressive."

Ava didn't return the smile. "What do you want?"

Evan took a slow step toward her, hands in his pockets.
"I want to make you an offer. One that makes more sense than the last."

Her pulse stumbled. "Evan, I told you—"
"Ava." His voice softened into sales-mode velvet. "You're overwhelmed. Behind schedule. The town may love your nostalgia, but nostalgia doesn't fix wiring that's decades out of code."

Ava tensed. He shouldn't know details.

Evan held up a sleek folder. "I represent a group that wants this corner for a modern café concept. They're prepared to offer..."
He opened the folder and slid a page toward her, "...a generous sum. More than before."

Ava's breath caught.
It was a life-changing number.
A walk-away-clean number.
A go-anywhere-start-over number.
Except... it wasn't her grandmother's bakery anymore if she sold it.

"Evan," she said carefully, "I'm not looking to turn this place into another chain."

His expression tightened. "Then look at the practical side. Your contractor may not have told you—but I've seen the structural concerns on this block. If this building is unsafe, it won't matter how much heart you put into it."

A chill raced down Ava's spine.
"How do you even know about the structural issues?"

He smiled, thin and sharp.
"I have connections with the city. Permits, safety records... those things pass across the right desks."

She felt suddenly small.
"You're trying to scare me."

"I'm trying to help you," he said smoothly. "Before you pour money into something that may not be salvageable."

A knock on the open door cut through the tension.
Declan stood there, jaw tight, gaze locked on Evan like he'd walked in on a threat.
"What's this?" Declan asked, stepping between them without hesitation.

Evan's smile sharpened.

"Hayes. Good to see you still... making do."

Declan ignored that. "Ava?"

She swallowed. "He came with another offer."

Declan's eyes flicked down to the number on the sheet.
A muscle in his jaw jumped.
He handed the paper back to her like it was contaminated.
Evan raised a brow.

"You should listen to someone who understands buildings,
Ms. Carson. That man may be good with his hands, but he's not
licensed to make structural safety assessments—"

Declan moved one slow step closer.
"Careful."

Evan glanced at the floor, unbothered.
"Just stating facts."

"You're stating things with motives," Declan said, voice like
gravel. "And none of them have to do with her safety."

Evan exhaled dramatically.
"Ms. Carson, this is only going to get harder. My offer won't
stand forever."

Ava's heart hammered so hard she wasn't sure she could
speak.
But she did.
"No."

Both men froze.
"I'm not selling," she said, stronger now. "Not now. Not later.
This bakery is staying mine."

Evan's expression flickered—annoyance beneath the charm.
"Very well," he said coolly. "But don't say I didn't warn you."
And he walked out.
The silence left behind felt electric.

Declan released a breath he'd been holding.
"You okay?"

Ava nodded, though her hands trembled.
"He knows too much, Declan. About the wiring. About the permits. I don't like it."

Declan stepped closer, his voice low.
"I meant it earlier. Don't trust him."

She searched his face.
"You think he'd actually sabotage this?"

His eyes hardened—more emotion than he usually allowed through.
"I think people who want something badly enough will do things they can justify later."

A small, nervous laugh escaped her.
"That's... comforting."

He gave a faint smile.
"Didn't mean to scare you."

"You didn't," she whispered.

But the way he was looking at her—steady, protective—made something flutter low in her stomach.
For a long moment, neither of them moved.

"Ava," he said gently, "you're doing the right thing."

She swallowed past the sudden tightness in her throat.
"I hope so."

Declan hesitated—like he wanted to say more—but instead he nodded and stepped back.
"We should check the wiring in the back today. Just to be safe."

She nodded, relieved and disappointed at the same time.
But something had shifted.

For the first time, Declan wasn't just the contractor.

He wasn't just the guarded man with careful boundaries.
He was someone on her side.

And Evan Rourke had accidentally done her a favor:

He'd pushed her and Declan onto the same team.

A team that felt dangerously like... *something more.*

CHAPTER 13

The back of the bakery smelled faintly of vanilla and cold air —
the kind that clings to a walk-in freezer no matter how many
boxes of flour and berries sit beside it. Ava balanced two bags
of frozen blueberries in her arms, nudging the metal door
open with her hip.

"Declan?" she called over her shoulder. "If you track more
sawdust in here, I'm going to start charging you a cleanup fee."

His voice floated from somewhere behind her, low and
amused.
"Add it to my bill."

She rolled her eyes and stepped deeper into the walk-in. The
blast of cold hit her instantly, raising goosebumps along her
arms. She set the blueberries on a shelf, shivered, and turned—
Just as the heavy metal door swung shut behind her.

Ava blinked. "Um—Declan?"

A click echoed.
A strange, sharp little sound.
She reached for the handle.
It didn't budge.
"Uh-oh."

Footsteps approached outside, steady and familiar. Then his
knuckles tapped against the door.
"Ava? Why'd you close it?"

"I didn't!" She twisted the handle again. Nothing. The air felt
colder suddenly — or maybe that was panic. "It's stuck."

"What?" His tone changed instantly. Sharper. A touch
worried. "Move back."
She did. The door jerked violently, once, twice. The steel rattled

against its frame, but stayed firmly, stubbornly locked.

"Damn it," Declan muttered. "The latch must've jammed when it slammed."

"Okay," she said, breath coming out in a thin white cloud. "Okay, well, you can fix things. Fix this."

"That's the plan."
But she heard the frustration under his breath.
And the quiet something else.
Concern.

A few more pulls — metal grinding against metal — then his voice again.
"Ava... it's not opening from the outside."

A flutter of worry tightened her chest. "So what do we do?"

"I'm going to call Eli. He's close — he can bring tools."
A pause.
"No service back here," he added, voice muffled.

She leaned her forehead against the cold door. "Perfect."
Inside the freezer, the air was cold but not unbearable. Still, she rubbed her arms, shivering.

Then:
Declan's voice softened.
"I'm right here."

Ava swallowed.
That helped more than she wanted to admit.
Footsteps outside, then the faint scrape of metal — he was sitting on the floor against the door. She could practically picture it: long legs stretched out, shoulders broad enough to block half the hall.

She slid down too, until her back rested against the inside of the door. Only a few inches of steel separated them.
"I swear this wasn't my fault," she muttered.

"I know." His tone gentled. "Freezer doors are temperamental.

They stick when they're old."

"Like you?"

A short laugh. "I'm thirty-two, not eighty."

"Could've fooled me."

Another laugh — deeper this time.
Silence settled, but not the cold kind. Something warmer.
Something that hummed between them.

After a minute, he asked quietly, "You okay in there?"

"Yeah. Just... chilly."

A beat.

"Wish I could get to you," he said under his breath.

Her pulse hit the roof.
She pretended she didn't hear that.
She absolutely heard that.
...

He scrubbed a hand over his face, trying to tamp down the sudden rush of heat that had nothing to do with the damn freezer.
She was right on the other side of the door.
Close enough that if he leaned back, he'd feel her warmth through the metal.
He shouldn't be thinking about that.
But he was.

He could picture her curled against the wall — cheeks pink from the cold, lips parted slightly as she breathed.
He hated that she was stuck.
He hated it even more that he couldn't fix it for her instantly.
And yet...
He didn't want to leave.

"Talk to me," he said, because silence felt too dangerous — like his thoughts might step out into the open.

"About what?" she asked softly.

"Anything."

He heard her shift — imagined her tucking her knees to her chest.
"Okay," she said. "Tell me something real."

He closed his eyes.
Real?
Dangerous territory.
But her voice — warm, hopeful, trusting — undid something in him.

"I like working here," he said.

She laughed. "Liar."

"I do," he insisted, lowering his voice. "I like... being around you."

Silence.
Long, honey-slow silence.

Then, very quietly:
"Declan..."

He pressed his head back against the door.
If steel weren't between them, he'd reach for her.
He wasn't sure he could stop himself.
...

Her breath caught.
The cold didn't matter anymore — she felt flushed, too warm, almost dizzy.

"Say it again," she whispered before she could stop herself.

"What part?"

"That you... like being around me."

He chuckled softly. "You want me to repeat it?"

"Yes."

The air crackled.

"Ava," he murmured, voice low and sincere, "I like being around you. More than I should."

Her knees wobbled. She sat down fully, heart pounding. "I like being around you too," she confessed. "More than I expected."

A slow exhale from the other side of the door. "Careful," Declan warned gently. "You're going to make this freezer a lot hotter."

Her breath hitched.
He didn't take it back.
He didn't laugh it off.
This was happening.

"So what now?" she whispered.

"Well..." His tone dropped another octave. "If you weren't trapped in there, I'd probably move closer."

"I'm already close."

"Closer."

Her heart flipped.
"Declan..." she breathed.

The door between them suddenly felt too thin. Too flimsy. She leaned back against it — could almost feel his weight mirroring hers.
For the first time, she imagined what it would feel like to turn around and meet him chest-to-chest.
Warm, solid, safe.
Too tempting.

"Are you thinking what I'm thinking?" he asked quietly.

Heat curled through her stomach. "Probably."

Heavy silence — charged, electric.
This was it.
This was the moment when everything could change.

Ava closed her eyes.
"Declan... I—"

Footsteps thundered down the hall.

"Hold on!" Eli shouted. "Got my drill!"

Ava's eyes flew open.

Declan swore under his breath — softly, almost regretfully.
The metal door finally screeched as tools worked at the
jammed latch. A loud pop, a jolt, then—
Light spilled in.

Declan was there first, pulling the door wide. His body filled
the frame, expression tense, eyes burning with something he
quickly masked.

She stepped out, heart hammering.

"You okay?" he asked, voice rough.

"Yes," she said, breathless. "Are you?"

A muscle jumped in his jaw.
"I will be."

Their eyes held — close, too close — until Eli cleared his throat
loudly beside them.

Declan stepped back.
Ava exhaled.
The moment was gone.
But not forgotten.
Not by either of them.

CHAPTER 14

Ava arrived at the bakery early the next morning, hoping the cool air and quiet would settle whatever was humming under her skin after... last night.

Locked in the freezer.
Chest to chest.
Breaths mingling.
Declan's hand brushing her jaw like he was memorizing it.
They hadn't talked about it.
They hadn't looked at each other long enough to try.

So when she walked in and found the workbench cleared, the broken lower cabinets fully repaired, and half the electrical outlets replaced, her stomach dropped.

"No. No, no, no..." She spun in a circle. "Declan Hayes, don't you dare."

Right on cue, he stepped out from behind the pantry doorway, wiping his hands on a rag. His T-shirt was smudged with white dust, and a tiny wood shaving clung to his hair. He looked maddeningly casual for someone who had clearly put in hours of labor she had never approved.

"Morning," he said.

She planted her hands on her hips. "What did you do?"

He blinked. "Fixed the outlets. Leveled the cabinets. Reinforced the—"

"Without asking me?"

His brows pulled together. "They needed to be done."

"I didn't authorize any of this, Declan!"

"It wasn't part of the invoice," he said calmly. "You're not being charged."

Ava stared at him, feeling heat rise in her cheeks — embarrassment, anger, and something else tangled together. "That's not the point."

"What is the point then?"

"That I don't want you fixing things behind my back like I can't handle my own responsibilities."

Declan's jaw tightened. "That's not what I'm doing."

"Really? Because it sure looks like you're trying to rescue me."

His voice lowered. "You think this is pity?"

"What else am I supposed to think? I am barely holding this place together. I can't afford half of what needs doing and you —" Her throat tightened. "You're swooping in trying to save me."

A long, tense moment stretched between them.
Then his expression shifted — not defensive, not irritated. Just... honest.

"Ava," he said quietly, "it's not pity."

"Then what is it?"

He stepped closer. Just one step, but it felt like the room leaned with him.
"It's respect."
Her breath caught.

"I see how hard you're fighting for this place," he said. "I see the hours you put in. How you don't quit even when everything goes wrong." His voice deepened. "People don't usually fight this hard unless it means something to them."

Her chest ached in a way she didn't know how to process.

He wasn't patronizing her.
He wasn't trying to save her.
He believed in her.

"Declan..." she started, softer now.

But before she could finish, the front door chimed.
A woman stepped in — tall, sleek ponytail, perfect makeup, sunshine-bright smile. Her fitted blazer screamed I know exactly how good I look. She carried a glossy catalog under one arm.

"Ava? Hi!" she chirped. "I'm Tessa from SweetPro Baking Supply. We spoke on the phone yesterday? I brought samples!"

Ava blinked. "Oh — right. Yes. Samples." She forced a polite smile.

Tessa's attention shifted... instantly... to Declan.
And lingered.

"Well," she said, voice dipping half an octave, "you didn't tell me there'd be a contractor here."

Declan nodded stiffly. "Just finishing up."

Tessa offered a slow smile, the kind Ava had seen women give men they wanted to flirt with. "Finishing up? Or starting something?"

Declan looked like someone had handed him a puzzle he didn't want to solve. "Just... working."

Tessa tucked a strand of hair behind her ear. "If we ever need renovation help at our warehouse, we could use someone with your... hands."
Ava nearly choked on air.

Declan cleared his throat, visibly uncomfortable. "I'm booked for months."

"Mm. Shame." Tessa's smile was syrup-sweet. "Here's my card anyway."

She slid it directly into his hand.

Ava felt a tiny, ridiculous spark burn in her stomach.
Jealousy.
Actual jealousy.
Declan noticed.
Because of course he noticed everything.

He stepped back like he needed distance. "I should pack up
my tools."

When he walked past Ava, she kept her expression neutral, but
inside her thoughts were anything but.
Why did she care if some flawless supply rep found him
attractive?
Why did it bother her when he barely reacted?
Why did it sting that he hadn't looked at her like that?

Tessa headed toward the display counter, flipping open the
catalog. "So! I brought icing samples, silicone trays, flavor
syrups—oh, and a 20% discount if you order before Friday."

Ava tried to focus, but her mind was still back near the pantry
door where Declan had said respect like it was something
sacred.

As Tessa rambled, Ava saw Declan in the reflection of the
bakery window — packing his tools slowly, shoulders tight,
expression unreadable.

He glanced at her.
Just once.
A single, restrained, charged look.
Then he turned away.
And Ava felt it — the shift.

The aftermath of almost kissing him wasn't fading.
It was deepening.

And whatever was happening between them was no longer
something she could ignore.

CHAPTER 15

By the time Ava arrived at the bakery the next morning, she
was still simmering with a quiet, embarrassed mix of jealousy
and irritation. She hated that a five-minute interaction with
the too-perfect baking-supply rep had set her blood buzzing
like that. And she hated even more that Declan had smiled at
the girl — actually smiled — a full, warm one Ava hadn't even
realized she'd been waiting to see again.

The bell over the bakery door gave a half-hearted jingle as
she walked in. Declan was already there, crouched by the
baseboards with a level in one hand.

He didn't look up.
"You're early."

"So are you."
Her tone was sharper than intended.

Declan finally turned. His brows rose slightly — that quiet,
assessing look he always gave her when she was pretending she
wasn't upset.
"You okay?" he asked.

"Fine."

"Uh-huh." He straightened, dusting drywall off his hands.
"Because you sound like you want to throw something at me."

Ava crossed her arms. "Why would I want to throw anything
at you?"

"Don't know." He shrugged. "Maybe I breathed wrong again."

Her cheeks flushed hot.
She turned away before he saw too much.
Declan watched her for another beat — the way she moved

too quickly, the way her shoulders tightened — and his own expression shifted, softening briefly before he masked it again.

He cleared his throat.
"The inspector's coming in an hour."

Ava froze. "Wait — today?"

"Yep. Last-minute call. They're trying to squeeze everyone in before the long weekend."

Great. Perfect. Exactly what her nerves needed.

She paced toward the front counter. "What if something's not up to code? What if they red-tag the whole thing? What if—"

"Ava."
Declan's voice was low, steady, cutting through her spiral.
She looked up.
"I won't let anything happen to this place," he said simply. "Not while I'm working on it."
Something inside her eased — just a fraction.

...

Inspector Dalton arrived with a clipboard, a gruff moustache, and the energy of a man who hated both small talk and smiles. He walked the perimeter, poking things with unnecessary aggression. Ava held her breath the entire time. Declan stayed close, quiet but watchful, interjecting only when Dalton reached for something dangerous.

At the breaker panel, Dalton frowned.
"This wiring's practically antique."

"I've already scheduled replacement," Declan said. "Parts arrive tomorrow."

Dalton grunted. "Hm."

At the back wall, he tapped on a support beam. Paid too much attention to it.

Ava's stomach twisted.

But Declan stepped in — literally stepping between her and the beam like he could shield her from bad news.
"That one's braced internally now," he said. "We reinforced it yesterday."

Dalton checked the bracket, hummed, scribbled. "Expected worse."

Ava let out a breath she hadn't realized she'd been holding. The whole inspection took thirty minutes, but her nerves felt like they'd aged a decade.

Finally, Dalton snapped his clipboard shut.
"You're not there yet," he said. "But you're on the right track." He looked at Declan. "Good work."

Declan nodded once.
Ava nearly sagged with relief.

When the inspector left, she leaned against the counter, exhaling hard.
"Thank you," she said.

Declan tilted his head. "For what?"

"For... not letting him terrify me. And for knowing what to say. And—everything."

He didn't reply right away. He just looked at her. Really looked at her.
It made her pulse flutter.
"I'm here to help," he said quietly. "Whether or not you believe that."

...

The moment of calm didn't last long.
An hour later, while Declan ran to his truck for supplies, a well dressed woman walked in; introduced herself as Emily. The woman had perfect curls, a blinding smile, and asked for Declan like she already owned a piece of him.
Ava folded her arms.
"He's not here right now."

Emily's smile tightened. "Oh. Well, could you let him know I found that color swatch he liked?”

Ava blinked. “Color swatch?”

Emily giggled. “He said it might look cute in *your* shop.”

Oh.
Oh, that traitor.

Ava managed a thin, polite smile. “I’ll pass the message along.”

Emily flounced out.

Declan came back two minutes later, hands full of screws and brackets.
“What’d I miss?”

Ava did not look at him.
“Your friend stopped by.”

He froze. “Friend?”

“You know. The one with the swatches.”

Declan stared at her blankly for a long moment — too long — before realization hit.
“Oh. Emily.” He groaned. “She’s not—Ava, she’s just a sales rep.”

“She’s very... enthusiastic.”

“She flirts with everyone. Yesterday she flirted with the building inspector. Dalton nearly quit the profession.”

Ava tried — really tried — not to laugh.
But a small snort escaped.

Declan looked relieved. “There it is. Thought I lost you for a minute.”

Her cheeks warmed. “I wasn’t... lost.”
“Looked like jealousy,” he said softly.

She nearly choked on air. "I was not jealous."
His mouth tugged. "If you say so."

Their eyes held a moment too long.
A moment with sparks.
A moment she felt in her ribs.
...

Later, while Declan worked on the back wall, Ava dug through an old set of drawers, trying to organize the last of her grandmother's scattered papers.
One drawer stuck badly. She yanked. It gave suddenly — and something thin, leather-bound slid out and dropped at her feet.

A journal.
Her breath hitched.
The cover was etched with flour dust and old fingerprints. She recognized her grandmother's handwriting on the first page.

She flipped through slowly, heart tightening at each entry — recipes, little notes, reminders, memories.
And then the final page.
The handwriting was shakier, uneven.
"If something happens... tell Declan."

Ava froze.
The whole room seemed to tilt.
Declan?
Her grandmother had known Declan?
She reread it — once, twice — but the words didn't change.
When she turned, Declan was still at the back of the bakery, shoulders tense as he hammered a bracket into place. The late-afternoon light caught the curve of his jaw, the quiet strength in him.

A man she was beginning to trust — and maybe want — far more than she should.
But now there was something she didn't understand.
Something bigger.
Something unsettling.
She whispered into the stillness:
"What exactly aren't you telling me, Declan?"

CHAPTER 16

Ava didn't remember walking back into the bakery. One second she was outside, air burning her lungs, and the next she was standing in the middle of the empty shop, surrounded by flour dust and silence. The familiar smell of old wood and sugar wrapped around her like a reminder she no longer deserved. This place had been her grandmother's heart—a warm, steady pulse in a small town. Now it was falling apart, and for the first time, Ava felt like she was, too.

Declan stood just inside the doorway, shoulders tense, jaw tight. He looked like someone bracing for impact, his breathing not quite steady, as if the words she'd thrown at him—You're fired—had knocked the air out of him.

"Ava," he said quietly. "Don't do this."

"Don't?" Her voice came out sharper than she meant, frayed around the edges as she grabbed the counter for balance. "You lied to me, Declan. For weeks. You let me believe you barely knew her, and all this time you—"

"I didn't lie." His tone was low, rough, and nothing like his usual steady calm. It sounded bruised. "I just didn't tell you everything."

"That's the same thing," she whispered.

His jaw flexed. He didn't try to argue.
For a long moment, neither of them moved. Dust floated lazily through the slant of morning light between them, softening the corners of the room even as the space itself felt sharp and painful.

Declan finally stepped forward, slow and careful—as if any sudden movement might make everything crack. He stopped well short of touching her.

"I should've told you," he said. "From the beginning. But she —your grandmother—she made me promise not to. She didn't want you thinking about anything bad when you left town. Said you already had enough on your shoulders."

Ava pressed her lips together so hard they trembled. "That's not your choice to make," she said. "You don't get to decide what I can or can't handle. You don't get to protect me from my own life."

A heavy silence dropped between them.

His eyes flicked downward, then back up. "I know," he said quietly. "And I'm sorry."

The apology cut deeper than the secret.

It would have been easier if he'd stayed defensive, if he'd shrugged and said it wasn't his fault. But the regret in his voice made everything worse, because it chipped at the anger she was clinging to like a life raft.

She shook her head, needing distance more than answers. "I can't think clearly with you here. You need to go."

He swallowed, throat working, and nodded once. "If that's what you want."

"It is," she said, even though the lie stung as much as the truth.

Declan hesitated for a heartbeat, like he was giving her one last chance to take it back. When she didn't, he turned and walked out, the soft thud of the door closing behind him echoing too loudly in the hollow space.

The bakery felt colder the second he was gone.

Ava stayed still until her legs started to shake. Then she sucked in a breath that didn't quite fill her lungs and pushed away from the counter. Motion. She needed motion. Anything to keep from replaying his face, his voice, that apology.
She started cleaning because it was something she could that

distracted her mind. Straightening chairs. Stacking pans. Wiping flour from surfaces that would never really be clean until the renovation was done.

When she opened one of the drawers behind the counter to look for a screwdriver to tighten a loose hinge, her fingers brushed something at the very back. Not wood. Not metal. Cloth.

Frowning, Ava reached in and tugged gently.
A folded bundle wrapped in a faded cloth napkin slid into her hand. The sight of it sent a ripple of unease through her.
She unwrapped it slowly.
Her grandmother's journal lay inside.

Not the one she'd already been reading in bed at night—the one that had worried her with that final half-finished line: If something happens... tell Declan. This one looked the same, but thicker somehow, heavier, like it had been waiting.

Her throat tightened. For a second she considered putting it back, pretending she hadn't seen it. But she'd already lost too many pieces of the truth.

She opened it to the most recent page she remembered reading—
—and her stomach dropped.

Everything after that familiar line was gone.
Not blank. Torn out.

The last intact sentence ended with tell Declan, and then the next page was a ragged stump, fibers frayed, edges uneven as if someone had ripped pages free in a hurry.
Ava's heart hammered against her ribs.

"No... no, no, no..."

She flipped forward, fingers moving faster now. Another section in the middle was missing, a whole cluster of pages clawed out. The journal felt mutilated, like someone had cut out pieces of her grandmother's voice.
Her pulse roared in her ears.

The entries right before the first torn section mentioned someone only as an initial:
D. stopped by today.
I worry he's in too deep.
If Ava knew...

A chill slid down her spine.
"D," she whispered. "Declan."

Her mind tried to rationalize it—*D could be anyone*—but the timing, the last page, the fact that Declan had been the last person to speak to her grandmother... it all tangled together in a knot of dread.

This wasn't random water damage or years of wear. This was intentional. Someone had not wanted these pages to exist. Her fingers shook as she flipped to the very back of the journal. There was a small pocket sewn into the inside of the back cover, a place she hadn't checked before. Something thin was tucked inside.

A folded slip of paper.
Her lungs forgot how to work.
She eased it open.
The handwriting was unmistakable—her grandmother's elegant, looping script.
Not everyone will protect what matters.
Trust carefully.

There was no date. No name. No explanation. Just the warning, sitting there quietly, like it had been waiting for the worst possible moment.
Ava stared at the words until they blurred. Her brain raced to stitch them to the missing pages, to the mention of "D," to Declan's soft apology and the way he had looked at her like she was breaking his heart and he had no right to stop it.
Had he read those pages? Had he seen this note? Had he removed them? Or had her grandmother hidden this from him too? Was he the danger... or the person she was supposed to be careful not to lose?

Questions twisted inside her, sharp and relentless.
A draft slipped through the front of the bakery and made the

bell over the door clink faintly, the sound oddly small in the quiet space. It felt, for an unreasonable second, like the building itself was listening.

Ava set the journal on the counter, palms flat on either side of it.
"I don't know what's happening," she whispered, voice shaking, "but I can't trust him. I can't."

Saying it out loud felt like a betrayal—of herself, of the version of Declan she'd started to believe in, the one who showed up early and stayed late and listened when she talked about cinnamon rolls and childhood and second chances. Trust was fragile. Hers had been cracked before. Now it felt like it had shattered clean through.

Her phone buzzed on the counter, making her jump.
A text from Declan.
Please let me explain. Please.
Her grip tightened around the edge of the journal.

Explain what, exactly? Why he'd never told her he was there at the end? Why he'd known her grandmother well enough to be mentioned in these pages? Why portions of those same pages were now missing? Why he'd been in and out of her life at exactly the right moments, always there when she needed help but never giving her the whole truth?
Or why her grandmother's last clear instruction had been tell Declan, followed by torn-out entries and a warning about trust?

Ava turned the phone face down.
"No," she said under her breath, the word barely steady. "No more."

But the moment the screen went dark, doubt pushed in harder. Because for all the warnings, for all the missing pages and unanswered questions, nothing in this bakery—no cracked tile or broken hinge or creaking beam—felt half as dangerous as how much she still wanted to believe that Declan could be the person who did protect what mattered.

And that was the part that terrified her most.

She looked down at the torn pages again, then at the note in her grandmother's looping hand. Everything she thought she understood—about Declan, about her grandmother, about why she'd been called back here now—had shifted.

The past was suddenly a puzzle with too many missing pieces.

And whether Declan was the villain of this story or the person trying desperately to hold it together... Ava knew one thing with absolute, painful clarity.

She needed answers.
Even if getting them meant risking her heart all over again.

CHAPTER 17

The storm rolled in before Ava even realized the sky had darkened, the kind of heavy, swollen clouds that felt like a warning rather than weather. She stood inside the bakery with her arms wrapped around herself, watching the first sheets of rain slap against the windowpanes. The old glass trembled with every gust of wind, and something inside her mirrored that shaking, a kind of fragile pressure she couldn't quite hold together anymore.

She'd tried pretending things were stabilizing. That the bakery was finally beginning to look like something living instead of dying. That she wasn't falling apart piece by piece as the past, the town, and Declan kept shifting the ground under her feet. But that illusion cracked the moment the wind began howling around the building, sharp and cold like it was deliberately hunting down the weak spots.

The first drip from the ceiling hit her wrist.
Ava flinched, staring up as water pushed through the plaster in a widening circle.
"No," she whispered. "Not today... please not today."

But the storm didn't care.
A second drip. Then a third. A slow, mocking rhythm.
Within seconds it became a steady stream, pouring directly onto the section of roof Declan had reinforced last month. The exact section she had insisted could wait for a proper fix. The decision she had made while still stinging with anger and heartbreak and suspicion.

Her fault. All of it.

A loud crack split the air, followed by the groan of shifting beams above her. Ava's breath caught. She backed away from the spreading puddle, anxiety climbing into her throat like something desperate and wild.

"I can't do this," she whispered, her voice breaking as the rain hammered harder. "I can't... I can't keep doing this alone."

The storm swallowed her words, drowning them in its fury. And then the front door swung open so forcefully the bell clanged against the wood.

Evan Rourke stepped inside.
Of course he did.

He brushed rain from his perfectly tailored jacket, looking around the room like he was already envisioning her bakery split into profitable square footage. His smile was soft, sympathetic—almost gentle—but too clean. Too prepared. Like he'd been waiting for the moment she broke so he could step neatly into the space left behind.

"Ava," he said quietly, as though soothing a frightened animal. "I heard there was damage here. Are you all right?" "I'm fine," she lied, wiping her cheeks with the back of her wrist. She wasn't even sure when she'd started crying. "It's just... a roof leak."

"A roof leak that could cost thousands," Evan replied, stepping closer. "And thousands you don't have. Let me help you."

"There's nothing you can do," she said, though the words felt unsteady, uncertain.

"Not true," he murmured, lowering his voice. "I can take this burden off your shoulders. I can buy the property today. Cash. No inspection contingency. No fuss. I'd preserve your grandmother's legacy in my own way, Ava. Her name would stay on the wall. I promise you."

A promise.
The word made her chest ache.

"Evan... I don't—"

"You're drowning," he whispered. "And you don't have to."
The bakery groaned under the pressure of wind, as if agreeing

with him. The ceiling dripped harder. A violent shudder went through the whole building, and Ava felt something inside her break open—fear, exhaustion, hopelessness.

Maybe he was right.
Maybe she was drowning.
And then, through the roar of thunder, through the claustrophobic weight in her lungs—
Another voice cut through the room.

"Ava! Don't sign a damn thing."
Declan.

He stood soaking wet in the doorway, rainwater dripping from his hair, his jaw clenched tight. His shirt clung to him like a second skin, plastered against the tension in his shoulders. And his eyes—God, his eyes—held something rawer than anger. Fear. Hurt. Something she didn't want to name but couldn't ignore.

"Declan," Evan said coolly. "You're interrupting."

"I'm stopping a mistake," Declan shot back.

Ava's pulse tripped. She hadn't seen him since she'd fired him. Since she'd told him she couldn't trust him. And yet here he was—hurt in his eyes, determination in every line of his body, and something almost desperate hiding under it all.

"I don't need help," she said, though her voice wavered.

"You do," he answered, softer now. "But not his."

Evan raised an eyebrow. "And why not? You've lost your contractor. Your roof's failing. You're clearly overwhelmed. I'm offering a solution."

Declan stepped forward, closer to Ava, like he couldn't stand the space between them.

"She's overwhelmed because she's doing this alone," he said. "Because people keep pushing her into corners she shouldn't be in."

A muscle ticked in Evan's jaw. "Is that what you call respecting her choices?"

"I call this—" Declan gestured to the leaking ceiling, the trembling floors, Ava's shaking hands— "a damn storm. And you're circling like a vulture."

Ava sucked in a sharp breath.
"Stop," she whispered, voice cracking. "Both of you. Please."

The storm raged above them. Rain pounded the roof with brutal force. Thunder vibrated the windows.

Evan stepped back, smoothing his jacket. "My offer stands, Ava. But it isn't forever. Think carefully." Then he slipped out into the storm.

The moment he left, the bakery felt bigger. Colder. Too quiet.
Declan didn't move.
He just looked at her.
Like he saw every fear she tried to bury.

"Ava..." His voice broke before the rest could escape.

"Why are you even here?" she whispered. "You don't work for me anymore."

"I know." His chest rose and fell unsteadily. "But you needed help."

"How would you know that?"

"Because I—" He stopped, jaw tightening. "Because I hear things. People talk."

"Talk about... what?"

Another beat of silence.
Then—

"The storm damage didn't start this," he said quietly. "The roof was compromised because the support beam shifted. And it shifted because someone removed a brace."

Ava froze.

"What are you saying?"

"That this wasn't an accident."

Her breath fractured. "Declan… who would do that?"

His eyes darkened, haunted. "Someone who doesn't want this bakery standing."

The room tilted under her feet.

"And there's more," he added, voice thick. "I wasn't just passing by today. I came because… I found something. Something about your grandmother."

"What?"

He swallowed—something heavy, painful.
Then, finally:
"She didn't just trust me, Ava. She asked me to protect this place. And you."

Her heart slammed against her ribs.
"But I didn't tell you because… I was afraid you'd push me away the moment you knew how much this mattered." His voice cracked. "And I was right."

The storm roared.
The bakery shook.
Ava couldn't breathe.
She didn't know whether to run to him—
or run from the truth he carried.

CHAPTER 18

Ava didn't know why she ended up at Mrs. Potts's front porch that afternoon. She only knew she couldn't stay in the bakery any longer without feeling like her ribcage was collapsing inward. The storm had finally passed, leaving the streets washed clean but quiet, the kind of quiet that felt like the world holding its breath. Maybe she needed someone who had known her grandmother. Someone who could help her make sense of the mess she'd made. Or maybe she just needed to hear that she wasn't losing her mind.

Mrs. Potts answered the door with her usual soft gasp of delight. "My heavens, Ava Carson. I was wondering when you'd stop pretending you didn't see me waving from next door every morning."

Ava tried to smile, but grief pulled too tightly at her mouth. "Hi, Mrs. Potts. I... I needed to talk."

The older woman's expression shifted instantly—gentle concern settling over her features like a shawl. "Well, come in, dear. You look like someone stole your sunshine and ran off with it."

Ava stepped inside, breathing in the familiar scent of lavender and lemon cookies. For a moment, she wanted to collapse into the safe warmth of it. Instead, she followed Mrs. Potts to the kitchen table and sank into the chair across from her. The table, with its chipped floral paint, had hosted half her childhood breakthroughs and breakdowns. Somehow, this one felt bigger than all the others.

Mrs. Potts poured tea, the clink of ceramic soft and steady, grounding Ava in a way she hadn't realized she needed.

"What's weighing on you?" she asked. "Your face has that look —same one your grandmother had the night she decided to repaint the bakery by herself and nearly set the ladder on fire."

Ava let out a shaky breath. "It's Declan."

Mrs. Potts didn't flinch, didn't look surprised. She just nodded slowly, like she had been waiting for this exact moment. "I wondered when you'd bring him up."

Ava pressed a hand over her eyes, feeling the exhaustion radiate through her skull. "I fired him."

Mrs. Potts inhaled sharply but said nothing.

"I didn't know what else to do. He kept secrets from me. Big ones. He was the last person to talk to my grandmother before she died. He never told me, and then—there were missing pages from her journal, and notes that sounded like warnings, and I just..." Her voice broke. She forced herself to keep going. "I didn't know who to trust."

Mrs. Potts took a long, slow sip of her tea before setting the cup down with deliberate gentleness.
"Ava," she said softly, "your grandmother trusted Declan more than almost anyone in this town."

The words stung—not because they were cruel, but because they were unexpected.

Ava blinked. "What?"

Mrs. Potts folded her hands on the table, her gaze steady and clear. "Declan helped her every week. Sometimes twice a week. Fixing shelves, checking the electrical, repairing the door when it stuck. She never wanted to bother you with the little things. She said you were building a life and she didn't want to pull you away from it."

Ava's breath caught, that familiar ache tightening across her chest. "She never told me."

"She wouldn't," Mrs. Potts said kindly. "She adored you, but she also knew how independent you are. She didn't want to worry you."

Ava exhaled slowly, her pulse beginning to thud in her ears. "Why didn't Declan tell me? He made it seem like he hardly knew her."

Mrs. Potts hesitated, then reached across the table and placed her wrinkled hand over Ava's. "Because your grandmother asked him not to."

A chill slid down Ava's spine.
"Why would she ask that?"

Mrs. Potts's expression softened with memory, with affection, with something deeper. "Because she told him something important. She said, 'When the time comes, when Ava is ready… watch over her.' Declan took that to heart. More seriously than any of us realized."

Ava's fingers curled against the table, her pulse thick and heavy. "Watch over me? That doesn't even make sense. Why would she—?"

"Because she trusted him," Mrs. Potts said softly. "And because she knew he'd be gentle with your heart, even when you weren't gentle with your own."

Ava's throat tightened so suddenly she had to look away. "I don't understand. I thought I understood him, but… everything is twisted now."

Mrs. Potts leaned back in her chair, her eyes warm and unbearably knowing. "You're looking at him through fear, not truth. And fear can make a good man look like a villain."

Ava squeezed her eyes shut. Declan's face flashed behind her eyelids—hurt etched into the lines around his mouth, disappointment shining in his eyes when she fired him, the way he hesitated at the door like part of him hoped she'd change her mind. She had pushed him away with more force than she meant to. Because she had been afraid. Because losing people had become a pattern she expected, not questioned.
Her voice broke when she whispered, "I hurt him."

Mrs. Potts reached over again, tapping Ava's knuckles gently.

"He's hurting now. But not because you fired him. Because he cares."

A shiver rippled through Ava at how certain, how absolute those words sounded.

"Declan doesn't let people close," Mrs. Potts continued. "Not since his marriage fell apart. But he let you close without even meaning to. That tells me more about him—and about you— than anything else."

A burst of warmth mixed with dread swelled in Ava's chest. "He should have told me the truth."

"Perhaps," Mrs. Potts said softly. "But ask yourself... would you have listened then? When you walked into town with your guard up and your heart wrapped in old hurts?"

Ava didn't answer. Because she didn't have to.

Something inside her shifted—like a wheel she'd been pushing against suddenly clicked into place. The missing journal pages. The warning. The silence Declan had kept at his own expense. It all blurred together into something she hadn't expected: He had been trying to protect her.

Not manipulate her.
Not deceive her.
Protect her.

Ava's chest tightened until her breath became a tremble. "I misjudged him."

Mrs. Potts smiled gently. "Then the question becomes... what are you going to do now?"

Ava looked down at her tea, her thoughts scattered, tender, undone. She didn't know how to fix everything. She didn't know what waited between them now—hurt, confusion, maybe something that looked like longing if she stared too honestly at it.

But she knew one thing with painful clarity.

"I have to find him," she whispered.

   Mrs. Potts nodded, as if she had expected nothing less. "Then go," she said. "Before you lose something your grandmother wanted you to have."

   Ava rose from her chair, her breath steadying with resolve and fear and something perilously close to hope.

Because for the first time, she wasn't just walking toward answers.
She was walking toward Declan.

CHAPTER 19

Ava didn't realize how fast she was driving until the tires crunched sharply over the gravel shoulder of the construction site. Her hands were trembling so badly she had to grip the steering wheel twice before she could force herself to turn off the engine. Even then, she sat there for a long, suspended breath, staring out at the half-framed house rising against the pale afternoon sky, feeling the weight of every mistake she had made pressing down on her ribs. Mrs. Potts' words still echoed in her chest with the ache of a bruise: He watched over your grandmother because she asked him to. He cared for her more than he ever admitted. And you... you were the reason he stayed.

Ava swallowed hard, the truth settling inside her with a complicated mixture of shame, hope, and something that felt terrifyingly close to longing. She had wanted to believe Declan was someone she could trust. And when she'd let doubt win instead... she'd broken something fragile between them.

She stepped out of the car, dust swirling around her boots, and scanned the worksite. Hammers rang in the distance, muted conversations carried across the churned-up ground, but her eyes searched instinctively for the one person who had filled too many of her thoughts for far too long.

She found him near the far side of the structure, kneeling beside a support post, sleeves pushed up, forearms dusted with sawdust and sunlight. He was focused, steady, every motion deliberate. It was strange how watching him work made her feel both grounded and undone. As if the world steadied around him—and she was the only thing trembling.

"Declan," she said softly.

He didn't move at first. Maybe he thought he imagined her voice. When he finally turned, the shift in his expression hit her like a physical thing—surprise first, then something guarded, something that might have once been warmth but was now barricaded behind caution.

"Ava," he said, standing slowly. "What are you doing here?"

"I needed to talk to you." Her voice was too small, too paper-thin for what she needed to say, but it was all she could manage.

Declan wiped his hands on his jeans, gaze flicking briefly to the flour smudged across her apron—she hadn't even noticed it was still on her. That tiny detail, the way his eyes softened for a heartbeat, nearly brought her to tears.

He stepped back, putting a careful distance between them. "I'm working."

"I know." She swallowed, pushing past the knot in her throat. "This won't take long."

The crew around them seemed to sense something tense lingering in the air and drifted to another part of the structure, giving them space. Ava clasped her hands together to stop their trembling.

"I talked to Mrs. Potts," she said gently. "She told me everything."

Declan stiffened almost imperceptibly, as though preparing for impact. "And what does 'everything' mean to you right now?"

"That you helped my grandmother every week. That she trusted you more than almost anyone. That you... were important to her." Ava lifted her chin, though her voice wavered. "And that she asked you to watch over me."

Declan looked away sharply, jaw flexing. "She shouldn't have said that."

"She trusted you," Ava whispered. "And I didn't. Not when it mattered. I'm so—"

"Don't." His voice cut through hers with more pain than anger. "Don't apologize unless you understand what you're apologizing for."

She stepped closer, ignoring the sting. "I do understand. I let fear twist everything into the worst version of you. I let a few torn pages convince me you were hiding something dangerous. I didn't stop to think that maybe... maybe you were the one person trying to keep the bakery standing. And trying to keep me standing."

His breathing faltered—just slightly, but enough for her to see the fracture behind his calm.

"I'm sorry," she said, fuller, steadier. "Not just for firing you. Not just for assuming the worst. I'm sorry for hurting you when you've only ever tried to help."

Declan dragged a hand over his jaw, exhaling like the words scraped something raw open inside him. "Ava... you didn't hurt me because you doubted me. You hurt me because part of me cared enough for it to matter."

Her breath hitched.

"And I tried to ignore that," he continued quietly, the gravel in his voice a mixture of restraint and confession. "Because you're leaving again one day. Because you have big plans, and I'm just the guy with a toolbox trying to keep an old building from collapsing. I wasn't supposed to..." He stopped himself, eyes shutting briefly. "I wasn't supposed to get attached."
The world stilled. Just him. Just her. And the truth hanging between them like a trembling thread.

"Declan... I don't want you to think you're 'just' anything." Ava took another step forward until she was close enough to feel the warmth of him, close enough to see the faint exhaustion in his eyes that had nothing to do with construction. "You're the only person who has shown up for me again and again, even when I didn't deserve it. You're the only one who hasn't walked away."

He didn't answer, but something in his posture softened—barely, but she noticed it.

She hesitated once... then reached out and lightly touched the flour smudge on her apron, drawing attention to it the way he had earlier. "You always notice the small things," she said with a shaky smile. "Even the things I miss."

Declan's eyes lowered to the mark as if pulled by gravity. Slowly—so slowly she barely felt it—he reached out and brushed the flour with his thumb. A ghost of a smile lifted at the corner of his mouth, subtle and reluctant and painfully tender.

"You're a mess," he murmured.

"And you always try to fix messes."

His gaze lifted to hers. Something warm and dangerous flickered there—something that felt like the beginning of everything she'd been afraid to want.

"Does this mean," he asked quietly, "that you want me back on the project?"

Ava nodded, breath unsteady. "Yes. But only if we do it together this time. No secrets. No walls. No disappearing when things get hard."

His thumb still rested against her apron, just above her hip. He didn't pull away. "And what about when things get messy between us?" he murmured.

Her pulse stumbled. "Then... we don't run. We figure it out." Declan studied her for a long moment, his eyes searching hers with an intensity that made her heart twist. Then he nodded, slow and deliberate.

"Okay," he said. "We finish the bakery together."

Ava let out a breath she didn't realize she'd been holding. Relief and hope mixed inside her, softening something bruised.

"And after?" she whispered.

Something moved in his expression—fear, longing, resignation, something aching and unspoken.

"We'll deal with 'after' when we get there," he said, voice low enough to shiver through her.

It wasn't a promise. But it was something alive. Something that could grow.

Ava nodded.

Declan stepped back, just enough to reclaim his breath, then reached for his tool belt.

"Come on," he said softly. "We've got a bakery to finish."

But this time, when she followed him into the half-built house, she felt something settle inside her—not certainty, not security... but the undeniable truth that this was the beginning of getting him back.

And maybe, just maybe, something more.

CHAPTER 20

Ava arrived at the bakery before sunrise, the sky still tinted with the soft lavender-gray of early morning, the kind of light that always made Maple Ridge feel like a place suspended between yesterday and tomorrow. She unlocked the door with a quiet breath, half-expecting the space to feel heavy with the memory of conflict—but instead, for the first time in days, she felt a fragile hum of hope stir beneath her ribs. Declan was coming back today. She had replayed yesterday's conversation at least a hundred times: the way his eyes softened when she apologized, the way he looked at her apron with that faint, devastating smile, the way something warm flickered between them like the wick of a candle trying to burn steady again after a storm.

By the time she slipped her apron on, the sound of a truck outside made her freeze. A familiar engine. A familiar presence.

Declan stepped inside without knocking—he never knocked—and something in her chest unspooled at the sight of him. His hair was still damp from a shower, curling slightly at the ends, and there was a new weariness around his eyes, as if the past week had carved itself into him just as deeply as it had carved into her. But he smiled—slow, cautious, almost shy—and it felt like sunlight cracking open a locked window.

"Morning," he said, voice low, warm.

"Morning," she breathed, surprised by how relieved she sounded.

He looked around the bakery, scanning the scaffold, the loose beams, the half-prepped workstations. "You started early."

"I couldn't sleep," she admitted. "I kept thinking... we have so much to fix."

Declan's gaze returned to her, steady and grounding. "We'll fix it. Together this time." He said the last part gently, as if he wasn't sure if he was allowed to hope for it.

Ava nodded, her throat tightening. "Together."

They fell into a rhythm so naturally it startled her. It was as if the bakery itself responded to their truce, the air feeling lighter, warmer, almost grateful. Declan set up ladders and tools while she cleared old debris. He cut new boards; she organized them by size. The silence between them wasn't tense anymore—it was full of a quiet, budding comfort, like two people remembering the shape of something they hadn't even known they missed.

At one point, while they were trimming replacement boards for the interior wall, her fingers brushed his when they both reached for the same measuring tape. The touch was small, hardly anything, but it lit a spark low in her belly—soft, electric, unmistakable. She pulled her hand back too quickly.

"Sorry," she murmured.

His voice deepened almost imperceptibly. "You don't have to apologize for touching me, Ava."

Her breath caught.
He didn't look away.
He didn't smirk.
He just... waited. As if giving her the space to choose what came next.

She forced herself to inhale. "Okay then," she whispered, her pulse skittering.

They went back to work, but something had shifted. The air felt charged, threaded with a tension that wasn't painful anymore—just warm and dangerous in the best way. When Declan moved behind her to reach for a board on the top shelf, his chest brushed her back and she had to close her eyes, steadying herself against the sudden wave of heat that rolled through her. He didn't apologize either. He didn't step away quickly. He just let the moment exist, a soft reminder of how close they had come to losing each other.

Around noon, Ava wiped flour from her cheek—she'd been testing cinnamon-roll dough again, experimenting with ratios —and realized Declan was watching her with a look that made her knees feel like they weren't entirely trustworthy.

"What?" she asked, trying to sound unaffected.

"Nothing," he said, but the faint smile tugging at his mouth told the truth. "Just... you look like yourself again."
The words hit her harder than he probably meant them to.

"Is that a good thing?" she asked quietly.

"It's the best thing," he said, just as quietly.

A moment opened between them—soft, warm, inviting—and Ava felt something in her chest tip forward, wanting. She looked down at the half-kneaded dough on the counter, then back up at him.

"Declan?"

"Yeah?"

She hesitated, pressing her palms against the cool marble to steady herself. "Would you... maybe want to stay for dinner tonight? Not fancy. Just... food. And company."

For a heartbeat, she worried she'd misread everything—that the tension was an illusion, that she was asking for too much too soon.

But Declan's expression softened in a way she had never seen before—unarmored, open, almost tender.
"I'd like that," he said. "A lot."

A small breath escaped her, almost a laugh, because relief mixed with something sweeter, something that felt like the beginnings of possibility.

"Okay," she said, trying not to smile too widely. "Then dinner it is.”

Declan nodded once, but his eyes lingered on her for a long moment, warm and intent, as if he was memorizing the way she looked when she was brave enough to choose him.

And Ava felt it, all the way down to the quietest parts of herself
—
the shift, the thaw, the truth she wasn't quite ready to name but couldn't deny anymore.

Something was starting.
Something real.
Something slow, and warm, and dangerous in a way that made her feel alive.

And tonight...
they wouldn't be avoiding it anymore.

Tonight, everything between them would begin to change.

CHAPTER 21

Ava hadn't expected to stand in her tiny kitchen feeling this nervous. It was ridiculous, she told herself, because she'd cooked a thousand meals in her life and none of them had ever mattered like this one. None of them had ever been for someone who made her heart trip over itself just by walking into a room. She kept smoothing her hands down the front of her apron, catching specks of flour and brushing them away as if cleaning herself up on the outside might settle the chaos moving inside her. But Declan's presence always did something strange to her—something warm and terrifying at the same time—and tonight was already shifting into a place she didn't fully understand.

When the soft knock came at the door, her breath caught. She opened it, and there he stood, shoulders filling the frame, hair damp from a shower, a clean gray shirt stretched across his chest like it had been waiting for this moment. He looked both rugged and uncomfortable, like he wasn't sure he belonged here, which only made something inside her soften in a way she wasn't prepared for.

"Hey," he said quietly, and the word seemed to settle into her bones.

"Hi," she breathed. "Come in. Dinner's almost ready."

He stepped inside slowly, eyes flicking around as if memorizing the details—her framed photos, the cookbook stack on the counter, the ceramic bowl her grandmother once made with her. When his gaze returned to her, something gentle flickered there.

"It smells incredible," he murmured.

"It's just roasted chicken and rosemary potatoes," she said, though her voice felt thinner than usual. "Nothing fancy."

He shook his head. "Ava... everything you touch turns into something warm."

The comment struck deeper than he probably intended. She looked away, heart thudding, and forced herself toward the stove before her knees betrayed her. They ate at her small table, candlelight flickering between them, shadows softening the edges of the room. At first the conversation was easy—gentle teasing, shared smiles, little fragments of stories she hadn't realized she wanted him to know. But eventually, the silences became heavier, weighted with something neither of them dared name too soon.

Declan pushed his plate back slightly, fingers resting on the edge as if bracing himself. "I owe you more honesty," he said quietly.

Her chest tightened. "Declan... you don't have to—"

"Yes," he interrupted softly, lifting his eyes to hers. "I do."

Ava leaned forward, every nerve alert. She had been waiting—hurting—wondering what parts of his past he had carried alone for so long. She watched him inhale slowly, like he needed the breath to steady the story inside him.

"There was a rescue mission," he began, voice thick. "A few years ago. My crew was called in after a building collapse. I wasn't supposed to go in—I was scheduled off shift because I hadn't slept—but I went anyway. I shouldn't have." He swallowed hard, the memory darkening behind his eyes. "Three people were trapped inside. We managed to get two out, but the last one... I reached him too late. He died before I could get him free."
Ava held her breath, her heart twisting.

Declan's fingers curled slowly against the table. "His wife came to the scene. I watched her fall apart while I stood there with dust all over me and... nothing to say. Nothing that would matter. And after that... I don't know. Something in me shut down. I quit the team. I couldn't carry someone's loss ever again. I couldn't risk being the reason someone waited for a door that never opened."

Her throat felt painfully tight. "Declan... you can't blame yourself for that."

"I do." He met her eyes, and the rawness there was almost unbearable. "Every day. Your grandmother... she saw it. She found me outside the hardware store one night after I moved here. I guess I looked as awful as I felt, because she didn't say anything—just put a hand on my arm and told me I was still needed. That I still had more good left in me than I realized."

Ava felt tears burning behind her eyes. "She always saw people that way."

He nodded slowly. "She asked me to watch out for you someday. Not because you were fragile. But because you were brave, and brave people sometimes forget they're allowed to be supported too."

Emotion surged through her so quickly she almost couldn't breathe. "Declan... why didn't you tell me all of this sooner?" "Because I didn't want you looking at me the way I look at myself," he admitted, voice cracking. "Like I'm made of all the wrong pieces."

She reached across the table without thinking, her fingers brushing his. His breath hitched almost imperceptibly, as if her touch fractured something in him he had been holding together too tightly.

"You're not broken," she whispered. "You're human. And you're good. And you've been trying to protect everyone but yourself."

His jaw tightened, a tremor passing through him. Ava stood slowly, moving around the table until she stood beside him. He looked up at her, something vulnerable and unguarded flickering through him.
"Ava," he whispered, as if her name itself hurt.

She lifted her hand, letting her fingertips trace the line of his cheekbone gently, like testing the reality of this moment. Declan closed his eyes, breath unsteady, leaning ever so slightly into her touch as if it grounded him.

Everything else faded—the candlelight, the ticking of the kitchen clock, the storm rumbling faintly outside. There was only the warm, aching space between them and the recognition that this moment had been building since the day she walked back into Maple Ridge.

When he opened his eyes again, they were softer than she had ever seen. "You make me feel like I'm allowed to breathe again," he said quietly. "And I don't know what to do with that." A slow, fragile smile touched her lips. "You don't have to do anything except let yourself feel it."

For a heartbeat, he didn't move. Then, with agonizing tenderness, he lifted his hand to her waist, his thumb brushing the fabric of her shirt as if memorizing the shape of her. She stepped closer, her pulse thundering in her ears, her hands sliding up to rest against his shoulders. His chest rose sharply with a breath.

"Tell me to stop," he murmured.

"I won't," she breathed.

Their foreheads touched first—soft, tentative, intimate. His fingers tightened at her waist, hers curled slightly against the warmth of his neck, the world narrowing down to the fragile, trembling closeness between them. When their lips finally met, it wasn't rushed or desperate. It was slow. Deep. A careful unspoken promise that whatever brokenness they carried, they were choosing this moment anyway.

He kissed her like she was something he'd been afraid to reach for, and she kissed him back like she was finally stepping into a place she hadn't realized she'd been searching for.

When they finally pulled apart, their breaths tangled in the small, quiet space between them.

"Ava," he whispered, voice unsteady, "I think this changes everything."

She smiled softly, brushing her thumb along his jaw. "I think it already has."

CHAPTER 22

The email came in the middle of a quiet morning, just as
sunlight was beginning to spill through the front windows and
turn the dust particles into something almost pretty. Ava had
flour on her hands and cinnamon under her nails, the familiar
comfort of dough resting under a tea towel on the prep table.
For once, the bakery felt... hopeful. Half-finished, still scarred,
but hopeful.

Her phone buzzed on the counter.

She wiped her hands on her apron and reached for it without
thinking, expecting a text from Declan about supplies or a
delivery or some small joke about how many times she could
rearrange the display shelves before he lost his mind.
Instead, she saw the name.

Evan Rourke.

Her chest tightened. He'd been suspiciously quiet since their
last encounter, and a tiny foolish part of her had hoped maybe
he'd lost interest. Moved on to another building, another town,
another person's dreams to rearrange.
Subject line: **Building Inspection Findings – 112 Maple Ridge**.

Ava's stomach dropped.

She hesitated for a heartbeat, thumb hovering over the screen,
then tapped.

The document opened in a blur of black text and red
highlights. Words like **structural compromise, load-bearing
concern, and unfit for occupancy without significant
intervention** stared back at her, circling her hope like vultures.
She skimmed, then went back to the top and forced herself to
read every line.
By the time she reached the last page, her hands were shaking.

It wasn't just a casual opinion or a half-hearted scare tactic. It was stamped. Signed. Official. The report claimed the building's foundational integrity had been compromised in multiple places and that prior renovation attempts had "failed to address core safety issues in a thorough or code-compliant manner."

There, underlined twice:
Recent work may have aggravated existing structural weaknesses.

Her vision blurred.
Recent work.
Declan's work.

Ava swallowed hard, throat painfully dry. She scrolled back to the beginning. Attached at the top of the email, beneath the formal report, Evan had added a short note.

Ava,
I'm concerned you haven't fully understood the risk you're taking. This building is not a fairy tale. It's a liability.
You seem like a smart woman. Walk away while you still can. I'm still prepared to make you a very fair offer before this becomes a bigger problem.
—Evan

Before this becomes a bigger problem.

Like it wasn't already devouring her from the inside out. The door at the front clicked, the bell chimed, and the sound made her flinch. She locked her phone, pressing it flat against the counter like she could smother its contents if she held it hard enough.

Declan stepped in, carrying a box of tools and a coil of new wiring over his shoulder. His T-shirt was already smudged with dust and something darker, and there was a faint cut along one knuckle, as if the morning had already demanded more from him than it should.

"Got the new junction box," he said, shutting the door with his boot. "If we swap this in and reroute the line, the lights will stop flickering like a horror movie."

Normally, she might have laughed at that, nudged his shoulder, made some comment about wanting customers who weren't afraid of being electrocuted buying muffins. Instead, her throat closed.

She just stared at him.

He stopped mid-step. His brows pulled together slowly as his gaze caught the tension in her shoulders, the way she held herself too still.

"You okay?" he asked quietly.
The concern in his voice almost broke her more than the email.

She forced herself to breathe. "Evan sent me something."

Declan's jaw tightened at the name. He set the tools down carefully, like he didn't trust his grip. "What did he say this time?"

"Not just words," Ava replied. Her voice sounded wrong to her own ears—thinner, frayed. "He sent... an inspection. A full report on the building."

He went very still.
"Let me see it," he said.

For a second, she didn't move, afraid that if she handed it over, everything would become real in a way she couldn't undo. Then she unlocked her phone with shaking fingers and held it out.
Declan took it carefully and read in silence.

The longer he stared, the more something in his face changed. The stubborn set of his mouth loosened, then hardened again. His brows drew in, then flattened. The lines at the corners of his eyes deepened, like every sentence carved a little more into him.

He got halfway through, exhaled slowly, then started over—this time more slowly, as if he was punishing himself with each line.

"Declan?" she whispered.

He didn't look at her when he answered. "This inspector...
he's not wrong about everything."

The words landed like a physical hit.

"So you knew?" Ava asked. "You knew the foundation was this
bad?"

"I knew it was rough," he said hoarsely. "I didn't know it was
this bad. Not from what I could see without tearing half the
place open."

He scrolled, thumb tightening around the phone. "Some of
this language is exaggerated. And some of it..." He shut his eyes
briefly. "Some of it's fair."

Something fragile inside her fractured.

"I trusted you," she said. The words came out softer than she
intended, but they still felt too loud in the quiet bakery. "I
trusted you when you said we could save this place."

His head snapped up then, meeting her gaze fully. There was
pain in his eyes—and something like shame.

"We could still," he said. "It would just take more money.
More time. More... everything."

"But what if we can't?" Her voice wobbled. "What if I've been
pouring every last bit of myself into a building that shouldn't
even be open?"

"Ava—"

"What if Evan's right?" The name tasted bitter. "What if the
safest thing is to sell it, let him bulldoze the memories, and be
done?"

The idea felt like betrayal, but so did standing here wondering
if she'd dragged Declan into a disaster he couldn't fix.
He set her phone down on the counter like it was something

dangerous. His shoulders were tense in a way she recognized now, something deeper than frustration—a withdrawing, shutting-down kind of tension that meant he was retreating inside himself.

"This isn't on you," he said. The words were quiet, but there was a rawness in them that scared her. "If anyone should've seen the scope sooner, it's me. It's my job."

She shook her head. "You're not an inspector."

"I'm supposed to notice things like this," he said, more to himself than to her. "I'm supposed to know where the weak points are before they break. That's the whole point. That's why people hire me."

His gaze drifted upward, toward the ceiling beams, as if he could see through them to every hidden flaw, every crack and shift and old scar in the wood.
"I missed things once before," he added, voice roughening. "Didn't see the problem until it was too late. People got hurt."

Her breath caught. She'd heard pieces of the story in fragments, in hints between his silences. A rescue mission gone wrong. A structure that hadn't held. The kind of memory that left shadows behind his eyes.

"Declan," she said carefully. "This isn't the same."

"Feels the same." His laugh had no humor in it. "I keep walking into broken things thinking I can fix them, and then I find out I underestimated the damage. That's on me, Ava. Not you. Not some developer with a report."

He took a step back, rubbing a hand over his face like he could scrub the guilt away.
"I should've pushed harder for a deeper inspection sooner," he said. "I should've insisted on a full structural assessment before we even touched the walls. But I... I wanted this to work. For you. For her. For all the things I didn't get right the first time."

Her chest ached. "So what now?"

He was quiet for a long moment. Too long.

When he finally spoke, his voice sounded like it had traveled a long way to reach her. "Now... I'm not sure I should be the one doing this."

Ice slid through her veins. "What are you talking about?"

"If this place really is as unstable as that report says," Declan said, nodding toward the phone, "you need someone who can give you every option, every angle, with zero history attached. No guilt. No promises to your grandmother. No... feelings." The last word came out strangled.

She stared at him. "You're saying you want to quit?"

"I'm saying I might not be what's best for the bakery," he replied. "Or for you."

"That's not your decision to make," she shot back. "You don't get to walk away because some old fear got kicked awake. That's not—"

"It's not just fear," he snapped, then immediately looked like he regretted the sharpness. He scrubbed his hand through his hair, shoulders rigid. "You think Evan sent this just to scare you? He's setting you up, Ava. If something does go wrong and he's on record saying the place is unsafe, who do you think they'll blame for touching it anyway?"

Her throat closed. "You."

"Yeah." His mouth twisted. "Me. The guy with the tools and the history. The guy who already wakes up thinking about the one time he didn't see the failure until he was standing in the wreckage. I can't... I won't put you through that. I won't risk you being inside this place if I'm not absolutely sure I can keep you safe."

Her eyes burned. "You're not keeping me safe, Declan. You're pushing me out."

He flinched.
Silence pressed in.

"I care about you," he said finally, each word dragged from somewhere deep. "More than I should, maybe. That's the problem. It clouds things. Makes me want to hope instead of calculate. And I can't do that when your life might be on the line."

Tears blurred the edges of her vision. "So your solution is to disappear? Again? Just like—"

He shook his head, cutting her off gently. "This isn't about walking away because it's hard. It's about stepping back before I make a mistake I can't repair."

"Maybe I get to decide if you're a mistake," she whispered. He looked at her then, really looked at her, like he was imprinting her onto his memory—the flour on her apron, the small streak on her wrist, the stubborn tilt of her chin even when she was breaking.

"I don't trust myself not to break you," he said softly. "And I couldn't live with that."

Before she could tell him she didn't need that kind of protection, that she needed him messy and flawed and present instead of perfect and gone, he stepped back.

He picked up his toolbox. His movements were gentle, careful, as if he didn't want to disturb anything else in the room.

"You should forward that report to another contractor," he said. "Someone with fresh eyes. Maybe two. Get a full picture before you decide anything. And... don't sign anything with Evan. Not yet."

"Declan—"

"Ava." His voice shook almost imperceptibly. "If I stay right now, I'm going to tell you it's going to be okay. That we'll figure it out. And I don't know that's true. I can't lie to you. Not anymore."

The finality in his tone terrified her more than any report. He walked to the door, opened it, then paused with his back to her.

"For what it's worth," he said quietly, "I never once saw this place as broken. Not really. Just… waiting. Like you." He swallowed. "You both deserve someone who isn't afraid of what might fall apart."

The words cut cleanly through her.

The bell above the door chimed softly as he stepped out into the gray, wind-streaked light. The sky had darkened without her noticing, clouds rolling in heavy and low.

Ava stood there, heartbeat loud in her ears, as the first rumble of distant thunder vibrated against the windows.

A storm was coming.
Inside the bakery, and out.

CHAPTER 23

Ava didn't sleep.

She lay awake with the inspection report on her phone, the ugly red "UNSAFE" stamp burned into her vision, Declan's empty expression echoing in her mind. The way he'd shut down, blamed himself, retreated. The worst part wasn't even the fear that the bakery might be unsafe. It was the way shame had settled over him like a second skin, as if every broken thing in her life belonged on his shoulders too.

By the time dawn filtered through her bedroom curtains, something inside her had shifted. The grief and panic were still there, but they were now threaded with something sharper, clearer.

Anger.
Not at Declan.
At Evan Rourke.

She sat up, grabbed her phone, and opened the report again. This time, she didn't just skim; she studied. Words and phrases stuck out at her—technical jargon she didn't fully understand, but some of it felt... wrong. It read less like a government document and more like a sales pitch for disaster.

If this structure is not vacated immediately...
Capital improvements would be unreasonable given the current state...
Owner strongly advised to consider demolition or sale...

Who "strongly advised" selling in an official report?

Her gut twisted. She might not know much about construction, but she did know one thing: the last person who'd pushed her that hard to walk away from something she loved had been her ex. And he'd used fear too—fear of failure, fear of embarrassment, fear of not being enough.

She'd listened then.
She wasn't going to listen now.

Ava swung her legs out of bed, grabbed a hoodie, and made coffee so strong it could've stripped paint. Then she dialed the number at the bottom of Evan's PDF.
The supposed inspector.

A clipped, professional voice answered. "Maple County Structural Services, this is Jenna."

"Hi," Ava said, forcing her tone steady. "I'm calling about an inspection report for the Buttered Biscuit Bakery. Issued yesterday?"

There was a quiet clicking of keys on the other end. "Address?"

Ava gave it.
Pause. More typing. Another pause.

"I'm not seeing anything in our system for that property," Jenna said.

A cold prickle crept down Ava's spine. "Could you check under the reference number? It's right here on the report." She read it off.

"Ma'am... that's not one of our formats," Jenna said slowly. "Are you sure this came from us?"

Her heart started pounding. "It has your logo. Your name. Your office address."

"We've had a few calls lately about fake documents using our letterhead," Jenna said, her tone cautious now. "Please send a copy of the report to our official email. I'll have our legal department take a look right away."

Ava's breath caught. "So you're saying... this might not be real."

"I'm saying," Jenna replied, "we did not send any inspector to

that property this week. And we do not encourage owners to
'consider sale' as a solution. That's not how we operate."

A tidal wave of fury rose in Ava's chest.

"Thank you," she whispered. "I'll email it now."

She hung up before her voice could crack.
Evan hadn't just pressured her.
He had faked an official inspection.
He had lied—to her, to Declan, to the entire town—just to scare
her into selling.
Something inside her snapped into place.
If he wanted a fight, he'd picked the wrong woman.
...

By midmorning, Maple Ridge's town square buzzed with its
usual Saturday energy—farmers' stalls set up, kids running
around with sticky hands, Mrs. Potts in her usual folding chair
like a small but unmovable queen. The air smelled like coffee,
cinnamon, and early spring.

Evan Rourke stood near the fountain, talking animatedly to
two shop owners, his designer coat somehow managing not to
catch a single speck of dust. He smiled the way men did when
they'd never had to wonder if anyone believed them.

Perfect.

Ava's heart pounded as she crossed the square. Her palms
were damp, knees a little shaky. But beneath the nerves there
was a new solidness. She wasn't walking away from herself
anymore.

She was walking toward the fight.

"Ava! Dear!" Mrs. Potts called from the side, but Ava lifted a
hand in a quick, apologetic wave.

"Two minutes," she mouthed.

This needed to happen first.

"Evan!" she called.

He turned with that polished, public-relations smile she'd come to hate. "Ava. You look tired. I'm guessing you saw the report."

His tone was gentle, almost kindly regretful. Like he was already consoling her.

"I did." Ava forced a matching smile that felt like it might crack. "Funny thing, though. The company on the report says they've never heard of my inspection."

His smile faltered.
Just a fraction, but she saw it.
A few heads nearby turned.

"A misunderstanding, I'm sure," Evan said smoothly. "You know how red tape is. Things get lost, delayed—"

"They also said," Ava continued, louder this time, "that they would never advise an owner to 'consider demolition or sale.' Or encourage them to walk away from a property onto which they'd poured their entire savings."

More people were listening now—Mrs. Potts, a couple from the café, the hardware store owner. Someone at a stall turned down their portable radio, and the murmuring of the square grew sharper, more focused.

Evan shifted his weight. "Ava, let's not do this here."

"You mean in front of witnesses?" she asked. "Yeah, that seems inconvenient for you."

His jaw tightened. "You're upset. Understandable. You're overwhelmed—"

"No." Her voice didn't shake this time. It rang across the open space, steadier than she felt. "What's overwhelming is you handing me a fake report to scare me into selling. What's overwhelming is you telling me you're 'just trying to help' while you undermine everything I'm trying to rebuild."

A low ripple of surprise moved through the circle forming

around them.

Evan glanced at the growing crowd, then leaned in slightly, lowering his voice. "You have no proof that it's fake."

"Oh, I do." She lifted her phone. "Emails. Names. Screenshots. I'd be happy to forward them to the mayor. And the county. And anyone here who'd like to know how you do business in their town."

Mrs. Potts' voice cut through from the side, bright and fierce. "I'd like to know. And I'd like to know how long you've been planning to flatten our bakery and slap some soulless chain café in its place."

Several people murmured agreement. Someone else added, "We don't need another corporate coffee shop."
The hardware store owner crossed his arms. "We like our town the way it is."

Color crept up Evan's neck. "You're all getting worked up over nothing. I'm offering investment. Jobs. Modernization—"

"At the cost of lying to one of our own?" Mrs. Potts scoffed. "Don't you dare stand here and act like that's charity."

Ava's eyes stung, but not from tears now. From the swell of voices around her. People she'd grown up with. People she'd once thought she'd abandoned. Standing beside her like she hadn't ruined everything just by leaving.

"I'm not selling," she said quietly, but the words carried anyway. "Not to you. Not now. Not ever. The Buttered Biscuit stays."

For a long moment, Evan just stared at her, the smooth veneer cracking enough for her to see the irritation, the calculation, the disbelief that she'd say no.

"This isn't over," he said softly, so only she could hear.

"Good," she replied. "Because I'm just getting started."

He pulled in a slow breath, forced that practiced smile back

onto his face, and turned away, retreating through the crowd as it parted stiffly.
No one stopped him.
But no one stopped watching, either.
...

Several yards away, half-shadowed under the maple tree across from the square, Declan stood with his hands shoved into his jacket pockets, jaw clenched so hard it hurt.
He hadn't planned to come.

He'd driven into town for supplies, intending to avoid Ava, avoid the bakery, avoid anything that felt like hope. But then he'd seen the small storm of bodies gathering, heard Ava's voice rise above the usual murmur.

And his feet had moved before his brain could stop them. Now he watched her, chest tight, as she stood in front of Evan like something unbreakable. This woman who'd once looked at him like he was the only steady thing in a collapsing world now held herself upright without him, shoulders set, eyes bright with fury and something more—conviction.

He'd read that damn report and felt every line like a personal failure. Missed rot. Missed cracks. Missed signs—just like before. It had pulled him straight back into that old nightmare, the one with smoke and sirens and too much weight in his arms and not enough time. He'd pulled away from her because he'd believed the worst: that he'd let her down all over again.

And yet here she was.
Not broken.
Fighting.
Because of course she was.

Declan watched the way people shifted closer to her—Mrs. Potts, the café owners, even Elias standing at the edge with his arms folded, nodding in approval. This town might have its gossip, its sharp edges, its smallness... but it took care of its own when it counted.

And she was theirs.
He swallowed hard, throat thick.

She's also yours, a traitorous part of him whispered. *If you weren't such a coward.*

When Ava said, "I'm not selling," something inside him loosened and tightened at the same time. Pride and fear tangled until he could barely breathe. He had wanted to be the one who made things safe for her, who kept the storms from getting too close. Instead, he'd believed a lie and let it send him running backward—again.

His fingers curled into fists. Old ghosts snarled at the edges of his thoughts—smoke, heat, a ceiling collapsing where it shouldn't have, a split-second miscalculation that had cost a man everything. He had dedicated every job since then to getting it right, to never missing a sign, to never being the reason someone's life came undone.

And yet with Ava, he'd missed something important—not in the beams or the wiring, but in the way fear could be weaponized. In the way a man like Evan could twist vulnerability into leverage.

He watched as the crowd slowly melted away and Ava stood with Mrs. Potts, shoulders sagging now that the adrenaline was bleeding off. Mrs. Potts reached for her hand and squeezed, and Ava leaned down to hug the older woman, pressing her face briefly into the soft curve of her shoulder.
Declan's heart clenched.

He wanted to be the one she leaned into. The one who held the weight for a while so her knees didn't have to.
Instead he stood beneath a tree, invisible.

His phone buzzed in his pocket—a text from the foreman asking if he was still coming by the lakeside job. He should. That was the plan. Keep his head down. Finish the contract. Forget the woman whose laugh had started living in his chest. But as Ava straightened and brushed her cheeks, as she turned toward the bakery with that stubborn, fragile determination he'd seen in her grandmother's eyes too, he knew he wasn't going to be able to stay away forever.

Not from her.
Not from the truth.

He watched her disappear up the street, the weight of his own choices settling heavier on his shoulders.

Ava had just stood in the middle of town and faced down a man who'd tried to control her life with lies.

If she could do that... maybe he could find the courage to face one more thing he'd been running from:
Her.

And the fact that, broken as he was, he still wanted to be the one who protected what mattered.

CHAPTER 24

The storm rolled in long before the town admitted it. Clouds stacked over Maple Ridge like bruised stone, heavy and threatening, the kind of sky Ava's grandmother used to call "a warning, sweetheart." The wind hit first, rattling the bakery windows, then the sharp crack of thunder followed, and the lights flickered as though the old building were afraid.

Ava stood in the center of the bakery, arms wrapped around herself, staring at the ceiling that had already betrayed her once. She had tried to be strong these past few days, had tried to pretend Declan pulling away didn't hollow her out in places she wasn't ready to face. But tonight the air felt different—charged, restless, cruel—and every corner of the bakery felt too big, too empty.

Rain slammed against the roof like fists.
A drip landed on her shoulder.

She didn't even have the energy to move at first. She just closed her eyes as another drip followed, then another, until she finally stepped back and looked up at the spreading dark patch forming overhead.

"Of course," she whispered. "Of course this would happen tonight."

Water began falling in earnest, hitting the floor in uneven taps. The storm outside howled, and the bakery groaned with the weight of it. A fuse somewhere snapped, and the entire building shuddered before going dark.

Ava inhaled sharply, forcing down the panic clawing at her throat.

She lit a small emergency lantern she kept on the counter and dim light washed over the empty shelves, the unfinished walls,

the raw beams still waiting for someone—Declan—to fix them.
The glow seemed to soften the room, but it only made Ava feel
smaller.

Everything was falling apart. And she was alone.

Her knees buckled before she could stop them. She sank to
the floor, hands covering her face as sobs tore free—quiet at
first, but then louder, shaking her shoulders until she couldn't
breathe.

She whispered into her palms, voice breaking.
"I can't do this anymore. I can't keep pretending I'm strong
enough. Grandma... I don't know how to save this place."

Lightning flashed through the windows, bleaching the world
white for a heartbeat.

She heard herself say it—words she had never allowed herself
to speak aloud.
"And I miss him," she choked. "God, I miss him."
•

Declan stood in the middle of the storm, soaked through,
heart pounding as he stared at the dim glow coming from the
bakery window. He had told himself not to come. Told himself
Ava needed space. Told himself he was doing the right thing by
staying away until he could breathe again.

But when the storm hit, something inside him snapped clean
in two.

He knew what these nights did to unstable roofs. He knew
how old buildings took pain personally. And he knew, without
any doubt, that Ava would be inside trying to handle it all
herself.
Lightning ripped across the sky, illuminating the street and
the shape of her car parked stubbornly beside the curb.

He swore under his breath.
"You're in there. Of course you're in there."

Guilt churned through him—heavy, sickening. He never

should've walked away. Not when she'd asked him to stay. Not when she'd looked at him like he was solid ground in a collapsing world.

Another bolt of lightning. Another crash of thunder. And the moment the bakery lights went out, Declan started running. By the time he reached the door, he was drenched from hair to boots. Rainwater streamed down his face as he shoved the door open without knocking.

"Ava?" he called out, breath sharp, chest tight. "Ava!"

No answer.
Only the sound of water dripping steadily from the ceiling.

He moved toward the faint glow of her lantern—and saw her. Kneeling on the floor, shoulders shaking, lantern flickering beside her like a dying heartbeat.

His own heart twisted so violently he had to grip the doorframe to stay upright.

She looked up at him with tear-streaked cheeks and eyes full of hurt. The sight nearly brought him to his knees.

He stepped inside in three long strides and dropped to the floor beside her.

"Ava," he breathed. "God—I'm sorry. I shouldn't have left. I shouldn't have—"

She shook her head, wiping at her face even though the tears kept coming.

"You did leave. And I don't... I don't know how to do any of this without you."

He reached for her, hesitated for a fraction of a second—then pulled her into his arms. She collapsed against him instantly, burying her face in his soaked shirt, fists curling into the fabric like she was afraid he'd disappear again.

The storm roared outside, but inside the bakery, everything went quiet.

Declan's voice was low, trembling with something that scared him more than the dark.

"I'm sorry I walked away. I thought... I thought I was the problem. That I kept hurting you by being here."

"You weren't the problem," she whispered into his chest. "You were the only thing helping me hold it together."

He closed his eyes, forehead pressing against her temple. "I'm sorry I left," he whispered again. "I'm not leaving again."

Ava let out a sharp, broken breath—a sound halfway between a sob and relief. She pulled back just enough to see his face, her hands sliding up to hold his jaw.

"You promise?" she asked, voice barely more than a tremor.

"I promise," he said. And for the first time in weeks, it felt like truth instead of hope.

Thunder shook the building. A loud drip hit the ground beside them. But neither of them moved.

Declan wiped a tear from her cheek with the softest touch.
"You're not alone in this. Not tonight. Not ever again if you'll let me stay."

Her lip trembled. "I want you to stay."

Something inside him broke open at those words—a dam of fear and longing and everything he'd been holding back to protect her. He cupped her face in both hands, his thumbs brushing warm paths along her skin.

"Ava," he said, voice roughened by everything he felt for her, "I mean this... I'm not going anywhere."

She leaned into him, her forehead resting against his, their breaths warm and unsteady between them.

The storm raged, the roof leaked, the bakery shuddered—but for the first time all night, Ava wasn't afraid.

He was here.

And he wasn't leaving.

Not this time. Not ever.

CHAPTER 25

The storm had passed by dawn, leaving Maple Ridge wrapped in a damp, trembling quiet. The bakery stood like it always did after a fight with the weather—wounded, but stubborn. Ava stepped outside for a moment, just long enough to breathe in the cool morning air and remind herself she wasn't dreaming. She had spent half the night soaked in tears and rain, convinced she had lost everything. And then Declan was there, breaking through the darkness like a force she no longer knew how to resist.

Behind her, the bakery lights flickered gently—running only because Declan had tamed the generator into cooperating. She turned back toward the door, heart tightening at the memory of how he'd stood there in the storm, rain dripping from his hair, breath coming hard, saying I'm not leaving again as if the words were scraped straight from his ribs. She wasn't sure she'd ever forget the way his voice had cracked.

Inside, she found him already working, his shoulders tense and damp beneath a clean shirt he must've kept in his truck. He stood under the newly braced section of the ceiling, staring up with the same haunted, determined expression he'd worn last night. There was something different in the air now— something quieter, softer, edged with relief but still shadowed by everything unsaid.

Ava stepped closer, letting her fingertips graze the edge of a bucket catching the last of the roof's dripping. "You didn't sleep," she murmured.

Declan didn't turn immediately. When he finally did, the exhaustion in his eyes was softened by something warm, almost grateful. "Didn't want to," he said. "Not until I knew the place was safe."

She felt her throat tighten. "You didn't have to stay all night."

His gaze held hers, steady and fragile at the same time. "I did. Because you were here. And I couldn't walk away from you again."

He said it so simply—so honestly—that something deep inside her loosened. She moved closer, slow enough to give him time to pull back. He didn't.

Instead, he reached out and brushed a strand of damp hair from her cheek. His hand lingered there, trembling slightly. "I thought I'd lost the right to stand here," he whispered.

Ava swallowed the ache forming in her chest. "You didn't lose anything," she said. "We were both hurting. We both made mistakes."

"No," he said gently. "You made a decision based on what you knew. I'm the one who kept too many pieces to myself."

She could hear the sincerity in him. It was the first time he'd ever sounded uncertain, vulnerable, almost afraid. She laid her hand over his. "Declan... last night you said something. I don't know if you meant it, or if it was storm panic, or—"

"I meant every word." His voice broke on the confession. "Ava, you make me want to stay alive."

The words struck her breathless. They weren't dramatic. They weren't poetic. They were simply true, born from a place he rarely let anyone see. She stepped closer until her forehead touched his chest, the rise and fall of his breathing grounding her. His hand slid into her hair, holding her gently, almost reverently.

"You saved me," he murmured into the top of her head. "You don't even know how much."

Ava closed her eyes. "You saved me too."

For a long, quiet moment they just stood there, letting everything soften—anger, fear, the mistakes between them. The storm felt far away now, but the intimacy it cracked open lingered in the air like electricity.

Eventually Declan drew in a breath and nodded toward the ceiling. "We should fix this before the inspector comes by again."

A teasing smile touched Ava's lips. "Are you sure? I thought you'd retired after last night's heroics."

Declan let out a soft, reluctant laugh—one that seemed to surprise even him. "If I retired every time a ceiling tried to drown us, I'd have quit years ago."

His humor warmed her more than it should have. "All right," she said. "Show me what to do."

They worked side by side, tools clinking in a gentle rhythm, the kind of shared silence that felt like trust instead of distance. Every so often their hands brushed, and each time Declan paused, just a fraction of a second, before continuing. Ava noticed. She felt every one of those micro-hesitations like a pulse of warmth in her chest.

When she climbed the ladder to help brace the beam, Declan steadied the base with both hands. "If you fall," he warned, "I'm catching you, but we're both going down with a concussion." She peeked down at him, smiling softly. "Then don't let me fall."

His grip tightened, knuckles whitening. "Never."

The word settled deep into her bones.
They worked until the ceiling looked less wounded, until the bakery seemed to hum with a fragile but real hope. When Ava finally stepped back to admire the progress, she felt something bloom inside her—a feeling she'd forgotten how to trust.

Declan stood beside her, his shoulder touching hers. "Looks good," he said quietly.
"It does."

He hesitated, then turned to her, voice barely above a whisper. "Ava... are we okay?"

She looked up at him, taking in the raw vulnerability etched across his face. "We're trying," she said gently. "And right now? That feels like enough."

He exhaled, long and unsteady. "I'll take that."

They stayed standing close, closer than necessary, until Ava's gaze drifted toward the small office where her grandmother's belongings were stacked. The journal sat on top of the box—mocking, mysterious, unfinished. She felt the weight of it again, heavy with questions she still didn't know how to ask.

Declan followed her gaze. "Is that what you were reading before... everything?"

She nodded. "There's more to it than I thought."

His shoulders tensed, but not with guilt this time—more like fear of repeating a wound. "If you want to ask me something— ask," he said. "I won't hide from you again."

Her chest tightened. "There are pages missing. Torn out. And some of the last entries were about you." She swallowed. "Declan... do you know anything about that?"

He went still, so still she could hear the faint hiss of the generator in the back room. Then, slowly, painfully, he shook his head. "No. I didn't know she wrote about me at all."

His voice was low, rough. "I would never destroy anything of hers. Not for any reason."

Ava searched his face—those eyes that always seemed to carry too much weight—and something inside her believed him instantly, instinctively. "I know," she whispered before she fully realized she did.

Declan closed his eyes for a moment in quiet relief, and when he opened them, there was a softness there she hadn't seen before. "Whatever she wrote... whatever you find... just know I would never hurt you. Or her."

She stepped closer until only inches separated them. "Then we'll figure it out together."

His breath caught. "Together," he echoed.

He touched her cheek again, gently, reverently, and Ava leaned into him, letting the moment stretch and settle between them—tender, warm, filled with a fragile certainty that something real was taking shape.

Outside, the morning sun caught the wet pavement, turning it gold. Inside, the bakery slowly came back to life, beam by beam, promise by promise, the storm beginning to fade into something they could survive—as long as they survived it together.

Ava reached for his hand. Declan threaded his fingers through hers.

They were officially together now.

And yet, somewhere in the back of her mind, the torn journal pages whispered their unfinished warning.

Trust carefully.
She planned to.
But she also planned to hold on to him.
For as long as he'd let her.

CHAPTER 26

Morning sunlight poured across Maple Ridge like it had been waiting for this day. The storm had broken sometime before dawn, leaving everything washed clean and shining—the sidewalks glistening, windows beading with leftover rain, the trees dripping quietly as if exhaling. Ava stood outside the bakery with her hands clasped tightly in front of her, her heart thundering against her ribs. For weeks she had imagined this moment, tried to picture it, tried to prepare for it. But nothing came close to the way it felt now: standing before a transformed building that held every memory she loved... and every new one she was ready to make.

The crowd gathering on the sidewalk felt unreal. Neighbors she hadn't seen in years. Kids holding tiny paper cups of lemonade. Mrs. Potts bundled in an oversized shawl, smiling like this was her granddaughter's wedding day. Even the mayor had come, though he'd tried—unsuccessfully—to blend in behind the balloon arch. Everyone was talking, murmuring, buzzing with a joy that lifted the air itself.

But Ava barely noticed any of it.
Her eyes kept drifting to him.

Declan stood beside her, dressed in a crisp shirt rolled at the sleeves, his hair still damp from the shower he'd rushed through that morning. He wasn't trying to stand out, wasn't trying to be anything more than the man who had helped rebuild this bakery—this dream. Yet he looked like the anchor in the storm, the steady thing her gaze couldn't let go of. His hand brushed hers once, almost accidental, but the warmth that shot through her nearly buckled her knees.

She swallowed hard. "I can't believe this is real."

Declan glanced at her, his expression softening in that way that always cracked something open inside her.

"You made it real," he said quietly. "You fought for this place. You brought it back."

"No," she whispered, her throat tightening. "We did."

A flicker of emotion crossed his face—part surprise, part something deeper, something yearning. And for a moment he looked away toward the freshly painted sign above the door, blinking as if he wasn't sure he deserved to be standing here beside her.

She nudged his arm gently. "You ready?"

He exhaled a small laugh. "I've been ready since the day that ceiling tile nearly took your head off."

A ripple of laughter spread through the front row—they'd clearly overheard—and Ava flushed. But the warmth settled into her chest rather than her cheeks. The town wasn't just excited. They were proud of her. Proud of what she'd resurrected. Proud that Maple Ridge had a heartbeat again.

The mayor stepped forward. "Ladies and gentlemen, Maple Ridge welcomes back the heart of our community... the bakery we all grew up loving. And thanks to Ava Carson—and a very dedicated reconstruction team—today we celebrate its grand reopening!"

The crowd cheered.

Ava's breath trembled. She reached for the ceremonial ribbon, her hands shaking slightly, and Declan stepped closer, his arm brushing hers, grounding her without having to say a word. She lifted the silver scissors, but before she could cut, the mayor paused.
"Ava, I believe you have something to say first."

Her lungs tightened. She hadn't planned a speech. She hadn't planned anything besides surviving this overwhelming swell of emotion.
She glanced at Declan. He nodded once—quiet, steady, believing in her more than she believed in herself.
So she tried.

"When I came home," she began, her voice softer than she intended, "I didn't expect to find the bakery in ruins. I didn't expect the dust, the broken beams, the storm damage, or the doubts." Her breath shivered. "But what I did find was something I never thought I'd get back... hope."

The murmurs softened. The town leaned in.

"My grandmother built this place with love. And I thought that when she was gone, the warmth of it was gone too." Her eyes stung; she blinked quickly. "But it turns out that home isn't a building. It's the people who show up when everything falls apart."

Her voice cracked at that, and she felt Declan's fingers brush the back of her hand—a silent promise she hadn't asked for but desperately needed.

"So today," she continued, swallowing hard, "I want to honor that. I want this bakery to be more than what it was. I want it to stand for second chances, and courage, and the belief that even broken things can be made beautiful again."

Declan's breath hitched—the tiniest sound—but enough to twist something deep inside her.

And finally, she lifted her chin toward the new sign covered with a burgundy cloth.
"I'm reopening this bakery under a different name," she said, her voice strengthening. "A name that reflects every journey that led me here."

She tugged the cloth free.
The crowd gasped.

In elegant gold lettering across the soft cream-painted board were the words:
THE OPEN DOOR

For a heartbeat, the world seemed to still—quiet, suspended, breathless.

Declan stared at the sign, then at her, something luminous and raw in his expression.

"You named it after... us?" he whispered, barely audible.

Ava's chest ached with emotion. "It's what you gave me, Declan. A door back to myself. Back to hope."

He swallowed, eyes darkening with something almost reverent. "Ava..."

But the mayor clapped loudly, jolting everyone back into motion.
"Let's cut that ribbon!"

Another cheer rose.

Ava lifted the scissors again, and this time Declan's hand slipped over hers—not guiding, not taking over—simply holding. Supporting. Steadying. The contact sent a warm rush through her entire body.

Together, they cut the ribbon.
The crowd erupted.

People poured through the doors, filling the bakery with laughter and wide-eyed wonder. Fresh pastries lined the counters, warm lights glowed from the fixtures Declan had hung himself, and the air smelled of cinnamon and citrus—the scent her grandmother had always said made a place feel like a hug.

Ava turned in the swirl of it all and found Declan watching her, his expression open in a way he rarely allowed.

"You did it," he murmured.

"We did it," she whispered back.

And then he stepped close—so close the noise of the crowd faded behind them. His hand lifted to her cheek, thumb brushing lightly as if memorizing the softness there. She leaned into him instinctively, her breath catching as his forehead pressed gently to hers.

"You're everything I never knew I was allowed to want," he

whispered, voice rough, almost breaking.

Emotion surged through her so intensely she had to steady herself with a hand against his chest.

"And you," she whispered back, "are everything I never thought I'd find."

He kissed her then—
Slow.
Full of gratitude.
Full of promise.
Full of all the open doors they were finally ready to walk through.

And when she pulled back just enough to breathe, she smiled —the kind of smile her grandmother would've called a beginning.

"Welcome home," she whispered.

Declan's answering smile was soft and full of wonder.
  "I am," he said. "Because you're here."

CHAPTER 27

Spring settled slowly over Maple Ridge, warming the rooftops, brightening the windows, and softening the edges of a town that had held its breath all winter. The bakery—her bakery— seemed to bloom with the season, its windows gleaming, its door freshly painted a warm honey-gold. People came in waves every morning now, each arrival a reminder that second chances, once fragile, could become something beautifully sturdy.

Ava had never worked harder. She had never laughed more, or cried more, or fallen so completely into a feeling she still didn't know how to name without her heart shaking a little. But it was real. And it was becoming something undeniable.

And every night, when the last customer left and the lights dimmed, she found herself staring at the door... waiting for the man who had become a kind of gravity in her life.

Declan stood there now, quiet in the doorway, dusted with late-evening sunlight. He held something small in his hand, turning it over like it mattered more than he knew how to say.

Ava wiped her hands on her apron and stepped closer. "You look like you're working up to something."

His smile was faint, almost shy, which still caught her off guard because she knew how much it took for him to let softness show. "Maybe I am."

She reached him, brushing a stray curl from her forehead as she searched his eyes. "What's in your hand?"

Declan exhaled slowly, then opened his palm.

A worn recipe card lay there, edges soft, ink slightly faded. But Ava would have recognized her grandmother's handwriting anywhere.

Her breath hitched. "Where... where did you find this?"

He didn't look away. Not this time. "I didn't find it. She gave it to me."

Ava stared at the little card—her grandmother's cinnamon roll recipe—but the back held something else. A note. A small, looping message Ava had never seen. Her heart pounded as she read the familiar script:
For Ava. When she's ready.

Emotion rippled through her so fast her vision blurred. "She trusted you with this?"

"She trusted me with a lot," Declan said softly. "More than I ever felt worthy of. And I didn't want to give it to you until... I don't know. Until you weren't looking at me like I might break your heart again."

She let out a trembling breath. "Declan... I was scared. I thought the missing pages meant something terrible. I thought she was warning me about you."

He stepped closer, close enough that the air shifted between them. "Maybe she was warning you about life. About trust not being something you hand out lightly." His voice dipped. "But she wasn't warning you about me."

Ava swallowed hard. "The pages... they still bother me. I don't understand why she tore them out."

Declan hesitated, eyes softening with a weight she hadn't noticed before. "I don't either. But I know she wanted you to find your way back here without feeling like anything was expected of you. She wanted your choices to be yours."

Ava traced a thumb over the recipe card. "It still feels like she's here somehow."

"She is," Declan murmured. "In this place. In you."

She looked up at him, and the ache inside her softened into something warm and full. "Declan..."

He took the recipe card from her gently and set it on the counter behind them, like placing something precious somewhere safe. Then he cupped her face with both hands, his touch steady, reverent.

"You know what this bakery taught me?" he asked.

"What?"

"That home isn't a place you inherit. It's a place you build. With someone who opens the door and lets you in."

Her breath caught. Every part of her felt suspended, pulled toward him like the moment before a storm breaks and everything becomes clear.

"This place opened more than a bakery," she whispered. "It opened me."

Declan closed his eyes for a heartbeat—like her words hurt in the best possible way—then leaned his forehead against hers. "Ava," he murmured, voice rough, "you make me want things I thought were impossible."

She slid her hands up his chest, gripping the fabric of his shirt, grounding herself in the steady rise and fall of his breath. "Tell me."

"I want to stay," he whispered. "I want to wake up knowing you're in my world. I want to build something that doesn't fall apart for once."

Her throat tightened. "You already are."

He pulled back just enough to look at her fully—eyes warm, vulnerable, certain.
Then he kissed her.
Slow, sure, deep enough that she felt it all the way down to the pieces of herself she hadn't realized were still broken. His hands slid to her waist; hers tangled in his hair. The world outside—the street, the customers, even the ghosts of old fears —fell away until there was only this moment, this man, this feeling that rooted itself with startling certainty.

When they finally broke apart, breath mingled in the quiet space between them, Declan brushed his thumb along her cheek.

"Ava Carson," he said softly, "every time you open that door, you walk toward me."

She smiled, tears bright and unashamed. "Then I'll keep opening it."

Outside, the newly painted sign swung gently in the breeze. *THE OPEN DOOR.*

Hope. Welcome. Home.

A love story written between torn pages, rebuilt beams, and the courage to forgive.

A future beginning every time the bell above the door chimed —and every time Declan reached for her, steady and certain, as if she were the place he'd been trying to return to all along.

One Year Later

The smell of cinnamon and warm sugar drifted into the cool morning air long before Ava unlocked the front doors. Maple Ridge still slept under a lavender-blue dawn, but The Door Back to You glowed softly from within — golden light spilling across the sidewalk like a welcome that never dimmed.

Ava stood inside the bakery, hands wrapped around a mug of steaming coffee, watching the sky lighten through the arched windows. She still had moments — quiet, unexpected ones — where the past tugged at her sleeve. Where grief felt like a soft thread woven through everything she loved.

But now, when she thought of her grandmother, the ache was warm, not heavy.

She smiled faintly.
She hoped she was doing her proud.

Behind her, footsteps approached, heavy and familiar.
A pair of arms slid around her waist, pulling her back against a solid chest that had become her safest place.

"Morning, Carson." Declan's voice was rough with sleep, and affection softened every syllable.

Ava leaned back into him. "You're up early."

"You're one to talk," he murmured into her hair. "I woke up, and you were already gone. I figured you were either baking... or plotting."

"Maybe both."

He huffed a quiet laugh, resting his chin on her shoulder. "This place looks beautiful."

"It's the same as last night."

"Yeah," he said, kissing her cheek, "and it was beautiful then, too."

A year of working side by side had left its mark — in the smooth rhythm they moved in, the comfortable banter, the sparks that still caught her off guard when his hand brushed hers. They'd repaired every inch of the bakery together, but somewhere in the sanding, painting, baking, arguing, forgiving... something inside both of them had repaired, too.

Ava turned in his arms, sliding her fingers into his shirt. "You know, when I reopened the bakery, I worried it wouldn't feel like mine."

"And now?"

She exhaled. "Now it feels like home."

Declan's expression softened — that breathtaking mixture of tenderness and something deeper he still struggled to name. "Good," he whispered. "Because you made it that way."

Ava kissed him, slow and lingering, her heart tightening in that familiar way that still surprised her.

When she pulled back, she brushed flour from his cheek — though he absolutely hadn't touched flour yet this morning. "You did that on purpose," she accused playfully.

"Maybe I wanted you to kiss it off."

"Declan."

"What? I like your solutions."

She laughed, pressing her forehead to his.

Then the bell above the door jingled as early customers trickled in — Mrs. Potts, bundled in her oversized coat; Elias with his morning newspaper; two teenagers holding hands like they'd invented love themselves.

Life filling the room.

Warmth returning in waves.

Ava stepped behind the counter and slid a tray of fresh rolls onto the display case. As she worked, she felt Declan watching her with quiet awe — like he still couldn't believe this was real. She understood.
She still felt that way, too.

Later, after the morning rush tapered off, Declan returned from the back carrying a small wooden box she didn't recognize. He wiped his palms on his jeans — a nervous habit she rarely saw anymore.

"Ava," he said, voice lower than before.

She looked up. "Everything okay?"

Instead of answering, he set the box on the counter between them.
Her breath stilled.
"Declan... what is that?"

"Something I've been working on." He pushed it gently toward her. "Open it."

The box was smooth, carved by hand, the grain of the wood warm beneath her fingertips.
Inside, beneath a layer of soft linen, lay a small stack of recipe cards — her grandmother's handwriting looping elegantly across each one.

Ava's throat tightened. "Declan... how did you—?"

"I restored them," he said quietly. "They were tucked in the back of her journal. Water-damaged, almost unreadable. I've been fixing them one by one."

Emotion blurred her vision.
She swallowed hard.

"You did this for me?"

"For you," he said, reaching out to brush a tear from her

cheek, "and for her. She trusted me with a lot. I don't plan to
fail her again."

Ava closed the box carefully, holding it to her chest.
"You never failed her," she whispered. "Or me."

Declan's jaw flexed — that old flicker of doubt — but he
breathed through it and met her eyes with something stronger.
Hope.

"Ava," he said slowly, "there's one more thing."

Her heart skipped.
He slipped a hand into his pocket — and her breath caught —
but instead of kneeling, he placed a small, folded slip of paper
on the counter.
It was old.
Familiar.
Her grandmother's handwriting covered the front.

Ava looked at Declan. "Where did you find this?"

"In the floorboard under the cupboard. Loose plank. I think
she meant you to have it."

Hands trembling, Ava unfolded the note.
*You'll know you're home when the person standing beside you
helps you open more than doors. — Love, Grandma*

Ava's vision blurred again, her chest swelling so full it almost
hurt.
She lifted her gaze, finding Declan watching her with a softness
she rarely saw — fierce, vulnerable, certain.

"I'm not asking you anything today," he said, stepping closer,
lowering his voice so only she could hear, "but I will. When the
time feels right. When you're ready."

Her pulse fluttered.

"And this," he continued, touching the note lightly, "felt like
your grandmother's way of saying... we're not far from that
moment."

Ava drew in a shaky breath.
   "Declan Hayes... are you proposing that you're going to propose?"

   A corner of his mouth curved. "Something like that."

She laughed — breathless, disbelieving, overflowing with love.
   "Well," she whispered, sliding her hands up his chest, "when the time comes..."

   He leaned in, his forehead resting against hers, their breaths mingling.

   "...don't keep me waiting too long," she finished.

   Declan kissed her, slow and sure — a promise wrapped in warmth and certainty.

   Outside, the bell chimed as another customer entered.
Inside, wrapped in golden light and the scent of cinnamon, Ava felt it in her bones:

She had finally found her way home.
And one day soon, when the next door opened...
Declan would be waiting on the other side.

ABOUT THE AUTHOR

Ava Larkson writes intimate, slow-burn romances filled with longing, hope, and the quiet moments that change everything. She lives in the United States, where she always has a notebook nearby— and a new story waiting at the edges of her imagination.

www.ingramcontent.com/pod-product-compliance
Lightning Source LLC
Chambersburg PA
CBHW020037310726
48970CB00007B/2289